The Worst Thing I Could Do

Kristy Lee

First Published in 2021 by Blossom Spring Publishing

The Worst Thing I Could Do Copyright © 2021 Kristy Lee

ISBN 978-1-8383864-4-3

E: admin@blossomspringpublishing.com

W: www.blossomspringpublishing.com

To my mom, Jean:

Thank you for supporting me through every chapter of my life.

A special thank you to my friend Rita Potter for her guidance during this process.

never go in search of love,

go in search of life,

and life will find you the love you seek - Atticus

Chapter One

The heel of my black boot taps relentlessly against the hard floor, provoked by the image of my apartment lit up in flames. A fire started thanks to the plastic from a melted comb dripping down the cord of the hot curling iron that I forgot to turn off; causing smoke to seep from the electrical socket, followed by a small spark that shoots and lands on my new perfectly folded lavender hand towel. One spark from one bad decision is all it takes for me to lose everything. With my imagination in flames, a distant sound sears its way through my brain, forcing me out of my head. It's Dr. Flanigan, and she is heated.

"Madeline? Madeline, did you hear me?" Her brown eyes are peering up from the rim of her dark glasses, irritation creating furrowed wrinkles between her brows.

"Sorry Dr., what is it?" A pink flush saturates my cheeks.

Chastising, she says, "This is really important for you all to hear so please pay attention. When you are conducting your research, you need to remain as professional and unbiased as possible. If you start to gain any sympathetic feelings for the inmates, then your analysis will become invalid. We need completely objective questioning, understand?"

"Yes," we all say in unison.

"Good, and, of course, this goes without saying, but becoming personally involved with an inmate will not only jeopardize the research and cost you your job, but it would also cost you your reputation. It is the worst thing you could do."

Tammy's plump, hairy-knuckled hand is in the air barely a second after Dr. Flanigan finishes her sentence, "Dr. Flanigan, I have a question."

"Yes, Tammy what is it?"

Tammy brings her hand down to cover her mouth, projecting a wet cough into it, then slowly wipes it with the back of her hand before responding.

"Don't you think it would be best if the women on this project didn't wear makeup to interview the inmates?" She knows darn well that I am the only one in this department who even wears makeup.

With an exacerbated eye roll, I retort, with sarcasm dripping, "I don't plan on wearing makeup to a prison Tammy, but thanks for your concern."

Tammy is determined to tick at least one person off each day and does a good job of it. Yesterday it was Dave when she not so subtly suggested that he was an idiot, by remarking about a study she read once that showed a correlation between cleft chins and low IQ. A remark that even Henry did not laugh at.

"Maddie, I am glad to hear that you already thought of no makeup. I wanted to let all four of you know some basic guidelines, including, no makeup, no tight-fitting clothes, no sexual innuendo, no real first names, no home addresses, and no giving out cell phone numbers. You will be interviewing extremely dangerous men, the last thing we need is for one of them to start writing you letters or calling you from prison. They do not need to know anything about you. This research is about them, not you. Make that clear. Be smart and safe."

For liability purposes, Dr. Flanigan is right to make this statement, but I am, of course, still offended. A neurotic sense of right and wrong would never allow for such a deviation to create any kind of personal relationship with an inmate. Plus, the promise of promotion after Dr. Flanigan leaves to pursue teaching, adds another element of importance to doing this job right.

Just yesterday, privately in her office, Dr. Flanigan dangled success in front of me, "Maddie, you are an excellent researcher and I believe you have the potential to be a great leader. I want you to take over for me when I leave. If you do an outstanding job on this project, I will write a recommendation letter to my boss. This could be your chance if you want it, Maddie."

"I want it, Dr. Flanigan. I want nothing more. This promotion is what I have always been planning for. A promotion would make me happier than anything else ever could." The sound from the beating heart in my chest increases with excitement.

"I don't know if a job is something that you should bank on making you happy Maddie, it is just a job. Happiness comes from within."

Whatever that means. Just give me the job lady.

"Dr. Flanigan? A quick question," Henry chimes in, his new light gray suit standing out against his dark skin, "will Dave have to have his chin searched when we go through security?" Laughs erupt from everyone except Tammy; her annoyance at why we would laugh at Henry's chin joke but not hers is evident when she puts

4

her hands up as if to say, "what the hell?" Tammy rarely pics up on social cues, the difference between a funny joke and an insensitive one lost on her like it always is, only fueling her general dislike for the human race.

"Okay everyone thanks for the laughs but that is enough for today. You need to get home and do some reviewing of the case files I have assigned you. They have details about each inmate you are dealing with, including their criminal history and any other background information we were able to dig up on them. I will meet you at North Branch Correctional tomorrow at eleven after you are done with your first day. Good night and good luck." Dr. Flanigan picks up her stuffed briefcase, pushes her glasses back up her nose, and marches out, leaving her expensive smelling perfume behind. Her life is so perfect; the perfect job, perfect-cropped hair, perfect pin-striped suit, perfect relationship with a perfect wife.

"Alright goodnight everyone," I say, trying not to linger on my envy of Dr. Flanigan.

"Yes, goodnight. Let's get some sleep so we can be prepared to sit with violent criminals for three hours. We need to be well-rested for that sort of thing. Should be fun!" I smile because even though Henry is being sarcastic, this should be fun.

Chapter Two

It takes a forceful turn to get the key to unlock the door of my apartment I got with the money from my divorce settlement. The emptiness of the dark space unfolds before me, mirroring the hollowness in my chest. My nightly ritual of setting my briefcase against the wall, then slipping off my long coat, placing it on the hook to the right of the designated key hook has become repetitious at best and monotonous at worst. I peel my feet out of my normally perfectly polished black boots, running my finger over a new scuff mark. Satisfaction comes from rolling my socks over the aching arches of my feet and stretching them against the cold, wooden floor. I grab my day planner out of my briefcase and open to the "to buy" section indicated by a purple sticky note and jot down "new pair of boots." I spend a moment admiring the color-coded sticky notes lining the edges, creating a symmetrical dream. It may seem strange, but this little planner brings me comfort, providing me with a sense of preparedness each day.

The bright orange sticky note on the front of the planner reading, "curing iron," in dark black ink, reminds me of the impending disaster in my bathroom so I sprint across the apartment. I flick the light switch on and my eyes dart around the room searching for melting combs and fires, only to find a curling iron that is, in fact, turned off.

"What's wrong with you?" I ask myself in the mirror; my freckles peeking through my foundation, taunting me like school children used to.

"Tilltot with all the spots" still rings in my ears. If only my last name did not rhyme with spot, perhaps I would not have hated my freckles so.

The gurgling in my stomach leads me to the fridge and I open it hoping it restocked itself. Thumping music shakes the wine glasses in the sink. The idiotic twenty-somethings would throw a party on a Wednesday night. Luckily, they are the only twenty-somethings that live in the complex; unluckily for me, they live in the apartment right next door.

Most of the people that live here are divorced professionals in their thirties and forties, the type of people who do not throw parties on weeknights. Instead, they sit and read or watch television, drowning out their loneliness with the stories of other people's lives. The people who live here are losers, some being here for years, roaming listlessly through their lives, never moving on to anything better. I will be on to better things and in a nice house again as long as I get the promotion. I hope to be out of this place in four months, totaling my time here in the lonely people's clubhouse for less than a year.

Do not get me wrong, I do not miss being married to my ex or anything, but my embarrassment by the divorce and my current living situation is undeniable. It is not like me to fail at anything and being a divorced thirty-something living in a place where single people go to die, was never in my life plan.

Yes, I have a life plan. One that I have been diligent about following ever since I was a young girl. Things just make more sense if they are planned for.

"Luck favors the prepared," was one of my mother's favorite things to say.

The life plan includes graduating high school with honors, going to New York University, graduating college with honors, meeting and marrying husband right out of college, having a successful career with the F.B.I, having two children before the age of thirty-seven, and being happy. I have accomplished everything on my list and am well on my way to having a long and successful career with the F.B.I., but the goal of having two children by the age of thirty-seven is in danger and the critical "being happy" seems to always be out of reach.

This life plan has served me well, being a beacon guiding me through all life's decisions. The only thing it did not prepare me for was my mother dying. No matter how much planning we did, nothing could stop her, or prepare me, for cancer. After I lost her, my determination to stick to my weekly, monthly, yearly, and lifetime plans solidified. In a way, it was to feel close to her. It was what bonded us, even after death. "I must follow the plan" was the mantra that rang in my head almost every minute of the day, leading some to call me "crazy" including my father.

"Maddie, your mother planned for everything, yes, but she didn't want you to forget how to live your life." I never really understood what he meant by that. Now, after ten years of arduously checking off goals since I lost her, my divorce seems to have driven a stake through the heart of my life plan, leaving me to try to resuscitate it.

The problem with having such a detailed life plan, like

a well-oiled piece of equipment, one wrench thrown into the mix can cause the entire machine to breakdown, and the next thing you know your life is in shambles.

Case in point: my apartment is not furnished. The few furnishings I do have include a small beige coffee table, a television, and two mismatched (yes, mismatched!) dining table chairs, and no dining table.

And of course, my refrigerator did not magically restock itself last night so I will have to call Chang's again.

"Chang's can I take your order?" says the exhausted man whose voice I have become all too familiar.

"Yes, I'm at North Street Apartment, number fifteen,"

"Ah yes, number fifteen, you want usual?"

Crap, maybe I am just like the losers that live here after all.

~~~

Blanche from the *Golden Girls* is making one of her typical conceited comments and, attempting to drown out the party next-door, I turn the volume up as high as it will go. While shoving beef and broccoli in my mouth, I flip through the assignment files Dr. Flanigan gave us desperately trying not to let the music and laughter distract me.

The three inmates assigned to me are Tyson P., Jonah M., and Freddy S. Each offender has convictions where robbery, violence and weapons were used during the commission of the crime. The youngest, Jonah M. is serving a thirty-eight-year sentence. What interests me the most about inmate Jonah M., is his age. Now at twenty-six, he is ten years younger than my other two inmates are. I am surprised Jonah M. was chosen because he does not have the long history of known violence that the other inmates we were assigned have. I remember that Dr. Flanigan mentioned that some of the original inmates that were asked to participate declined so I suspect Jonah M. may have been a second or even a third choice.

I quickly scan the mugshots to familiarize myself with their faces. When I get to inmate Jonah's picture, I am surprised. His dark blond hair is disheveled and just long enough to cover the top half of his ears. His green eyes appear sad due to a slight turndown at the outer corners; the sharp jawline cuts the softness of his other features. The flitting thought that he is quite attractive runs past my mind's eye before ducking behind walls of sensibility. A check of the time and I see that it is already two a.m. and the party next door has finally calmed down, allowing me to turn off the television and crawl into bed.

Pulling the comforter up to my chin, I shut my eyes, but I am too nervous to rest, tossing and turning probably a hundred times before drifting into an uneasy sleep.

Chapter Three

It is a Thursday morning in the middle of February. It is so cold out that a thick layer of frost has engulfed my car. The frozen ground crunches beneath my feet, while thick gloves are making it hard for me to grip onto the thin credit card that I use to scrape the windshield. My eyebrows scrunch in annoyance at myself for not being more prepared for these winter months. The card pushes the frost up, accumulating chunks at the end. I give up and climb into the car, turn on the heat, and wait.

My teeth are chattering so hard I worry they might break. Breath escapes my mouth in a plume of vapor, reminding me of the smoke from a cigarette, taking me back to the few rebellious drags I had in college. My wild days were very mild, with a few cigarettes and only a handful of late nights at parties being the extent of it. My best friend, Min, was always telling me that I was "missing out" as she lived her college days on the edge, relying on prayer and copious amounts of caffeine to make it to classes on time after partying all night. Partying was never my interest, well-organized girls with Type-A personalities such as myself do not fare well at parties, spending most of the time planning for how they will get home. Min was never burdened with these types of worries and I was always envious of her devil-may-care attitude. She has epic stories to tell, and I leech onto them as if they were my own.

These gloves and scarf are doing nothing to keep me warm while the car whines against the cold as if trying to tell me, it can no longer handle the agony of how I have been treating it.

I brush off the white balls of lint on my gray suit that is slightly baggy. I bought it online years ago and never wear it but, today, I have created the ideal body for a woman walking into a man's prison. One of no discernable shape whatsoever.

Perfect.

I wrap myself in my trusty thick winter jacket that I've had since I graduated from college and opt for Chapstick and a thin layer of foundation. I consider not wearing any foundation but am unable to overcome the pervasive insecurities about my freckles even when confronting criminals.

The car finally warms up enough that the frost has started to drip away; I swipe my windshield wipers once over, sweeping even more off so that I can see just enough to drive. I back out of the parking spot and begin the fifty-minute journey to the prison. My heart is beating fast, and I chew on my bottom lip. I have been to prisons before when I was completing my internship for my master's degree but have never spent one on one time with anyone dangerous.

"You are a strong, professional woman who will not be intimidated by anyone. You can do this Maddie. You've got what it takes."

I repeat this mantra; building up courage as I drive.

~~~

I finally pull into the prison parking lot and spot the rest of the team huddled together clutching their cups filled with coffee, white clouds escaping from their mouths. At least there is some distance between my apartment and the prison because the ice just finished melting off my car; saving me from the embarrassment of my colleagues thinking that I do not know how to take care of myself in these harsh winters.

"Hey Maddie, the last one here has to buy us coffee next time," Dave chatters against the cold.

"Of course, I can't believe I'm the last one. Am I

late?" I try not to sound horrified, but I have never been late to anything in my entire life.

"No, we just drive faster," says Dave, while handing me a coffee cup, "three sugars and two creamers, right?"

"Oh my gosh, thank you. You're truly a lifesaver. So, are we ready for this? Should we review our fake names, so we don't forget? I'm going by Sarah."

I choose Sarah because it is a simple, common name and I hope this will make it easy to remember so that I can react quickly if someone calls me by it. Moreover, it was my mother's name, but I keep that secret to myself.

"Sure, I will be Todd, Dave is Brad, and Tammy is Peggy. Now let's get in there. I'm freezing my butt off." Henry turns and leads the way into the prison and I quickly drink down the warm liquid, hoping the heat will radiate through my entire body.

We plan to reconvene back in the parking lot after three hours, with one hour dedicated to each inmate. My phone says it is eight a.m., so I set an alarm for eleven-thirty, giving a little extra time to go through security. We walk in and, just as I predicted, security takes a full thirty minutes to get through. We sign off on some documents and have our briefcases searched by the guards. We meet briefly with the head of security who gives us a safety rundown.

"You're set up to meet with the inmates in empty holding cells per the request we received."

We made this request because we want inmates to feel they are in a safe, anonymous space to encourage them to tell their stories.

"A guard will be posted outside of each cell and will be available if you need help."

The guards have their arms crossed over their chests and I spot one roll his eyes to another, perhaps we are an inconvenience. They fail to laugh when Henry suggests they do a full cavity search of Dave's chin, leading Dave to give him a "that's not funny anymore" face.

Walking behind the guards as they escort us to our cells is surreal; a flush of inmates uttering horrifying comments at us heightens the sense of danger at being around people who are not acting as if you expect people to. A raw, animalistic sensation surrounds me as the weight of the difficulty of this project sinks in my chest.

Guard Eric stops first in front of cell 3B and Henry motions me to use it.

"Go ahead and take this one, Sarah," he says in a low

voice, "it's closest to the exit." I nod as a subtle way to say thanks.

I step into a cell that contains a single gray metal table with two, also metal, chairs. Other than two bottles of water on the table, the room is empty with only a window to break up the barren walls. The small, barred up window serves no purpose, obstructing the view of the courtyard outside. I pick a seat and open my briefcase; my heart beating against my chest. I set the tape recorder, pen, and yellow notepad on the table in front of me.

After several minutes, the guard reappears with an inmate in front of him. The man standing in front of me is very large, maybe two hundred pounds, and sturdy. His bicep alone is larger than my skull. His orange uniform creates a stark contrast to the gray of the room.

As I stand to greet Tyson, he gives me a once over, cocks an eyebrow, and says, "You're doin' this?"

I gather myself, "Yes. Hello Tyson. My name is Sarah, and I will be working with you. Please have a seat," I say as I motion to the chair on the other side of the table.

Tyson sits and lets out a sigh, "I'm not real interested in talking 'bout crime to a girlie."

"I'm the person you are assigned to Tyson. Let's get

started, you can always back out if you want, this is completely voluntary."

During our hour-long session, Tyson does his best to intimidate me by staring me down and making blatant glances towards my chest. My palms become sweaty as I force myself not to break eye contact.

Tyson leaves and I wipe my hands on my pants and breathe a sigh of relief. The next inmate is Freddy. Freddy may be smaller than Tyson, but I preferred Tyson. Freddy's face is grim: his eyes empty, with a whiff of cruelty behind them. While he speaks loudly about his participation in the Aryan Race Gang, the artificial light overhead shines off the top of his shaved head, illuminating a swastika tattoo.

You can do this Maddie, I think to myself, almost believing it.

Freddy ignores most of my questions and spends the session rambling which is not helpful to the research. Freddy exits the cell and I breathe again. These are not going well, so I write a note that three one-hour meetings are not enough time spent with these inmates. It may take more time to be able to gain their trust and therefore provide something meaningful.

Inmate Jonah M. is next, and I am anxious to get this over with, my energy balls up in my shoulders, tightening them. I hear the guard bring Jonah in while I am still taking notes in my yellow notebook, so I do not immediately lookup.

"Sorry, have a seat, I'll just be a second," I gesture across the table to the chair.

I quickly finish my notes and look up to greet the inmate; doing my best to regain any amount of energy that I have left. Inmate Jonah is leaning back in the chair, looking down at his cuffed hands that he folds in his lap. He lifts his eyes to meet mine.

Wow.

He is more than just attractive; he is quite breathtaking. His green eyes are reminiscent of the color of freshly cut grass; the bright florescent light above us illuminating small flecks of gold in his irises. His messy hair is pushed back with a few loose strands falling across his forehead. He looks like his mugshot only harder, with a dusting of facial hair and slight wrinkling on his forehead. The time in prison has taken a visible toll, however, barely diminishing his beauty. He is the type of guy that women jump to fall in love with over, and over again, even though they knew it was a bad idea.

This could be a problem.

A small voice at the back of my neck reminds me to speak. "Oh, I'm sorry . . . um . . . hi Jonah, my name is Sarah." I sound like a stuttering fool.

Even as I say the name, Sarah, it feels awkward. It is wrong to lie to him about something as simple as a name, but to expect him to tell me the truth about the complex reasons behind his life choices. He looks at me quizzically and I think he might know I have given him a fake name.

Shoot, I thought I was a better liar.

His voice is deeper than I anticipated with a twinge of a southern drawl as he says, "Let's do this then."

I go through the spiel that I went through with the other two inmates, "Jonah, as you were previously instructed, this is voluntary and the information you share will remain confidential. There is nothing to gain from doing this; we are simply trying to learn from you, and you can back out at any point."

He is watching the words fall from my mouth with razor-sharp intensity; piercing me as if he is trying to see into my soul. My sweating increases and I am so glad that

I wore a dark gray suit. I shift in my seat trying my best to appear undisturbed. Some of the light from outside has made its way into the room, shining between the bars on the window, mirroring them onto the surface between us, spreading like fingers. The dreary image reminds me that I am in a prison, sitting across from a very dangerous man, someone I cannot afford to be attracted to. It is enough to jolt me back to reality, so that I may forget his looks and get through the rest of our interview with my professional demeanor intact.

The interview is made more difficult however, because, unlike my first two inmates, Jonah is not eager to talk. He is quiet and only answers the questions I have for him with simple one-word answers. This is going to be tough. Once the time is up, Jonah stands, and the guard leads him out by the arm.

I mutter, "Thank you, I'll see you next week Jonah," he looks back at me with some unreadable expression; marked by a tight jaw and thin, pursed lips.

Once he is out of sight, my shoulders drop from a sudden release of tension, and I gather my things quickly.

With all three sessions are over, I meet up with the rest of the team in the parking lot for a debriefing.

"This sucked. One of my guys said he refuses to meet with a woman and has decided to drop out." I am surprised anyone would think of Tammy as a woman, but I digress.

"Well, the men I met with didn't give me much of anything. They're more interested in trying to figure me out," Dave says with a dejected shrug.

I interject, "I don't know how much we are going to be able to get from these men with only three one-hour sessions. I mean, I think we need to factor in gaining their trust first. That may take longer."

"Oh great, so you want to spend more time with these people?" Tammy quips.

Henry jumps in "Yeah, I think you're right. These men are our research subjects, we need to invest the time needed to get the information we are looking for, or it will be all for nothing."

Thank you, Henry.

Dr. Flanigan pulling into the parking lot in her red Subaru. I used to think her car did not match her personality but then I learned that she spends her time hiking with her wife Lisa on the weekends and so it began to make more sense since Subaru's are common amongst the outdoorsy type and, of course, the professor type.

Dr. Flanigan is rubbing her hands together as she walks up and proclaims, "Oh my gosh it is freezing out here. I'm so sorry I'm late, I got held up at the office for a bit. Have you been waiting long for me?"

"No, it worked out well Dr. Flanigan, we needed extra time to get through security," I say as I glide Chapstick over my cracked lips. I really hate winter.

"Oh good, well there is a coffee shop across the street, should we reconvene over there?" We all nod in agreement, as I jump up and down desperate to warm myself up.

Once we get inside, we order and sit at a corner table out of earshot of the other patrons. Our much-needed coffee warms up our hands and throats as we begin to discuss the day. I start by repeating my concerns about the limited time we are spending with these individuals.

Dr. Flanigan reassures us that it might take a couple more sessions than we originally thought, in order to gain the inmates' trust, "Look, it is normal for research projects to change as we learn more factors that could hinder the research. We can change the outline of this project so that we can spend some more time with these men. It is best to do it now before we get in much deeper."

We spend the next thirty minutes discussing each inmate, and when it is my turn, I hesitate, "All three of mine were very different, but none of them gave me anything useful…the last inmate I met with, Jonah M., might be the most challenging for the research because he did not say much at all."

"I'll listen to the recording Maddie and see if we need to drop him or not."

"Okay, thanks Dr." That would solve one problem, now I just need to get used to meeting with criminals every week.

Chapter Four

Speeding down the highway on my drive back home, the gray sky and icy white snow whip by me in a blur. I want to do well on this project; I want to exceed expectations. I always strive to exceed expectations; it is my greatest attribute. A familiar sense of profound loneliness starts to seep back into my consciousness as I drive towards an empty home. This is a sensation that has haunted me ever since my mother died. I have tried dedicating my life to following my detailed life plan because it seems to be the only time the loneliness subsides. The life plan was supposed to fill me with accomplishments, purpose, love, and happiness, yet, here I drive, emptier than ever. Maybe this research project, the success of it, and promotion will finally do the trick, creating meaning and happiness in my life. The fear that no matter what I do, I will never be happy creeps in, and as I grip the steering wheel, my knuckles are as white as the snow.

~~~

Thanks to loneliness, the image of Jonah drifts into my thoughts as I lay in bed. I push him away by repeatedly reminding myself that I am a professional, I am not the type of person to find a convict even one iota, attractive.

Right?

I begin to spiral and ask myself, "Are you really so lonely that you think a violent criminal is attractive? Geez, Maddie. Get a grip."

Being a reasonable and practical person is something that I take pride in so what the hell is wrong with me? I contemplate reaching out to my therapist when my phone buzzes. It is Min and she wants to stop by, but I have been avoiding having her come over ever due to the state of my unfurnished apartment. Min knows me better than anybody and it will be immediately apparent to her that I am not myself when she sees how I have been living.

She is persistent, "Maddie, I haven't seen you in weeks and it is only nine o'clock. What are you? An old lady? Get up and I can be there in twenty."

I roll my eyes, "Okay fine, I'm getting up."

"Great! Be there soon!"

Even though I do not want her to see my apartment, it would be nice to talk with her about this research project and the inmate. Maybe she can knock some sense into me.

Within twenty minutes, Min barges into my apartment without knocking, wielding a bottle of Moscato. She is her usual beautiful self, flashing her toothy Julia Roberts-like grin. She, annoyingly, takes excellent care of herself and works out every day. Min's husband Raymond is incredibly lucky to have won the heart of someone like her because he is the kind of person you forget about as soon as he leaves the room. However, they have the type of marriage that seems almost perfect. Of course, it helps that Min makes sure to demonstrate their perfection on her very popular lifestyle blog and Instagram account that focuses on Korean beauty. While I normally believe that most people on social media are simply facilitating a façade that does not have a fraction of reality, I can honestly say that Min's is genuine.

As she sets the wine on the counter, Min glimpses at the state of my apartment and I recognize the look of horror on her face immediately.

"Maddie, you doin' okay? This place does not match your normal anal self. Is this why you haven't let me come over since you moved in?"

"I know Min. I don't know what is wrong with me, and yes, of course, I didn't want you to see this place. I hate it here."

"Have you considered going back to therapy?"

"Yes, I've been thinking about scheduling an appointment with Dr. Abby again, but enough about me, what's new with you?" I say, desperate to change the subject.

She gives me that 'sure' face and then quickly launches into how her daughter Lizzy got into a fight at school and her teacher, Mr. Patrick, thinks that Lizzy needs to learn self-control. This makes Min mad because she thinks Lizzy is just spunky. An hour goes by quickly as we talk and laugh. I finally get up the courage to tell her about my day.

Min is all over me when I bring up inmate Jonah, "What do you mean he is attractive? Like actually attractive or you are just losing it attractive?" Her brutal honesty stings.

"I don't know. It could be me. I have his picture if you want to see it."

"Duh," she responds.

As I hand her the file with Jonah's picture in it, I find I am hoping she also thinks he is attractive, and I am not just losing my mind.

To my relief, she says, "Oh wow, you're not kidding."

"What do you think I should do Min? Should I ask Dr. Flanigan to replace him on the project? I can't have any kind of biases within my research."

"And just how would you do that? What would you say? Oh Dr. Flanigan I have the hots for one of my inmates so can we use someone else?" She exclaims while dramatically waving her arms in the air. "You'd lose all credibility Maddie, don't be stupid," her dark eyes providing me with a mirror reflecting my stupidity.

I had not considered how I would explain the situation to Dr. Flanigan and suddenly become very grateful I ran this by Min, before I said something I would regret.

"Oh man you're right; I can't say that to her. I'm just being silly. I did tell her that he didn't open up at all during the interview, which is true, so there is a chance he'll be removed from the project anyway. Even if he isn't, I won't let his good looks impact my job. I have to do well on this project because Dr. Flanigan said that if I did, she would write a recommendation letter for me to be nominated for the promotion. Can you believe that? I might be getting my dream job Min."

"Wow, she said that? Amazing and I'm not surprised

at all Maddie. You work harder than anyone else I know." Min smiles and I know she means it. She is always rooting for me.

She stays over for another hour and grills me about how crappy my apartment is and why I am taking this divorce so hard.

She keeps repeating, "You cannot plan for every detail of your life Maddie. Divorce happens. Failed relationships happen. I know you have never failed at anything, but it just means you are human. Quit beating yourself up about this. It's not healthy."

"I know Min. I just can't seem to get a grip. I think this promotion will do it and I'll feel like myself again."

"That's a lot to put on a promotion Maddie. Maybe a job isn't all that you need. Maybe you need to just have a life instead."

"What do you mean? I have a life." Kind of.

"Maddie, I have known you since freshman year and I have never, not once, seen you have fun. You know what fun is right? It's that thing you do just because you enjoy it. It makes you laugh. You do know how to laugh right?"

"I laugh!" Sometimes.

"I know you laugh Maddie; you laugh with me. We

have fun together. However, a person should have more fun than just when they are hanging out with their best friend. You should try doing new things. Get outside your box a bit, hell do something spontaneous for once."

I decide to ignore such nonsense, she means well but I know what I need and "fun" will certainly not lead to a promotion. I am relieved when Raymond comes to pick her up, no longer wanting to be lectured. When she walks out the front door, she stumbles, grabbing the railing for support. The wine seems to have affected her mobility. I giggle slightly; a drunk Min has always been one of my favorite things and I have not seen her like this since college.

I wave to Raymond and mull over everything Min said. I regret having her see my apartment and for telling her about inmate Jonah, I do not confide in many people and when I do, I normally regret it. While lecturing myself about how ridiculous I am, I fall into a soft, wine drunk sleep while hugging a bag of Cheetos, orange cheese flavoring sprinkling my sheets and fingertips, something that I will chastise myself for in the morning.

Chapter Five

It's Friday morning and my head is pounding. I get some strange looks from my coworkers; I look down and see that my shirt is falling out of my trousers on one side. My cheeks are on fire as I tuck in the rest of my shirt.

Several cups of coffee later, I am finally able to contribute to the discussion at hand.

"Let's add two more interview sessions but why don't we each just continue the research with one of each of the three inmates? The one that is the most promising research subject?" Henry says jotting down ideas on a dry erase board.

"I like it, Henry. Why don't we increase the interview time of the last two sessions as well? Maybe spending a bit more time with them during those?" I say this with trepidation.

"How about two hours each?" Tammy says this while trying to wipe up the coffee she spilled on her brown blouse.

"No way, too long," says Dave, immediately cutting down Tammy.

"No, wait Dave. I like it. Think about it. That will

allow a longer time for them to get into their stories. Perhaps only an hour at a time isn't enough," Dr. Flanigan interjects.

"You're right Dr., that's exactly what we need," Dave always agrees with anything Dr. Flanigan says.

We spend the rest of the day working out the details, with changes made to the length of the plan and adding to the list of interview questions. Of course, these changes mean that I will be spending additional time with one inmate.

I just hope it is not inmate Jonah.

By the end of the day, we are all ready to go home, and Dave and Henry are discussing weekend plans.

"Man, I'm stoked. I just joined a league at my gym and will be playing b-ball every weekend. If you want Henry, I can get you on it too." Dave may be talking to Henry, but I notice he is looking at me. He has been looking a lot at me lately, but I brush it off as nothing.

"Na, I'm too old to play in a league. I don't move as well as I used to. I'm looking forward to treating Tamesha to date night though. I'm taking her to some ice-skating rink. It'll be romantic and hopefully lead to some lovin.' She hasn't put out yet, so I'm hopin' this will help."

Hearing about Henry's potential for a sex life is frustrating; it has been so long since I have been intimate with a man that I am starting to worry I forgot how.

"I don't need to hear about that Henry. This is a workplace." Tammy spits this out as though she is deeply offended. I roll my eyes.

"We're off the clock Tammy so get over it. We're all adults here and I wasn't talking to you anyway." Tammy pushes her chin and nose in the air as she saunters out the door.

"Geez, she's a piece of work. At least we have you, Maddie. You're chill. How's it going by the way? What do you have going on this weekend?"

Unlike the others, I do not look forward to the weekends because I do not enjoy my free time. Back when I was married, my ex and I would keep busy with fixing up our lovely home and having dinner parties with his colleagues. In fact, we were so busy, we never slowed down, never spent any time together just the two of us, or any time alone. I credit this as one of the reasons we fell apart. Now, post-divorce, I am always trying to avoid being alone by either going to the gym, shopping, or doing anything that keeps me distracted. By the time Monday rolls around, I am always grateful to escape the melancholy, listlessness of my lonely life.

This is not something I share with anyone; I do not expect to gain any cool points by bragging about how much I love work, hate the weekends, and have no social life.

"Oh, you know full plate. Going to a concert with Min."

"Awesome, what concert?" Dave asks as though he plans on joining.

"Nobody you would know. See you both on Monday," I say this while practically running out the door, so I do not have to be asked any more questions.

Chapter Six

"How was the concert, Maddie?" Dave asks and I give him a confused look, "Didn't you say you were going to a concert with Min? How was it?"

Oh yeah. *CRAP.*

"Yeah, sorry I didn't hear you at first. It was good, we had fun. What about you? How was the league?" I say this, desperately trying to change the subject.

"Awesome, the team has some pretty cool guys on it. Some I have never met before including one that is newly single if you're interested, Maddie." Dave raises his brow at this as if testing me.

"Oh gosh, me dating? I don't seem to have much luck in that department, and I don't want to be set up on some blind date. Thanks for thinking of me though."

Dave appears more satisfied with my response than he should be.

I sit to get to work, turning on my computer when Dr. Flanigan stops me, "Maddie I finished going through your recordings from the other day and I share your concerns about inmate Jonah M. He only gave one-word answers and didn't seem willing to open up to you all.

This could be a waste of time with him but let's give him one more chance and see if he talks more this week. If it does not get better this week, we will assign you a new inmate, you would need to go back to the prison a couple more times than planned."

"Sounds good, Dr. Flanigan. I will let you know if it gets better after I meet with him on Thursday. I don't want to waste my time either." I also do not want to meet with him if I do not have to, but I keep that thought to myself.

~~~

The rest of the week flies by and it is Thursday already again. I try not to think about it too much, but I am dreading heading back to that prison, but if I want this promotion, I must keep my discomfort to myself.

Before we walk through the large, metal gates of North Branch, Henry provides the pep talk, "Okay everyone, let's go in there and gather some data! Yay for criminals! Otherwise, we wouldn't have jobs!"

Dave shoots me a half-smile as Tammy rolls her eyes.

Once in cell 3B, I meet with inmate Tyson first. Unfortunately, for the research, Tyson spends this session bragging to me about his crimes instead of answering my questions about his background. Attempting to get him to tell me something more meaningful, I urge him to move away from the crimes and discuss his childhood.

"Can you tell me about what your childhood was like Tyson?"

Tyson leans his head to the right and gives me his best back-off face, "I don't wanna talk about that."

Yes. I have hit a nerve and make a note on my yellow notepad. It is a different reaction during the session with inmate Freddy who seems to enjoy talking about his childhood.

He boasts about how poor he was and how horrible his father was, "I would sleep on the floor of the crack house my dad sold drugs out of; bugs would scurry across my body all night long, creating paths up and down my bare legs. Once I got old enough, I joined the South Side Gang because I could crash at their place and get away from the crack house."

Freddy's gang affiliation is in his file, so I knew this was a large part of his life.

"How old were you when you joined the South Side Gang Freddy?"

He rubs his cracked knuckles as he utters, "Ten."

My heart aches as he says this, not for the scary man sitting before me, but for the young child that he once was.

It is time to meet with inmate Jonah and I nervously hope that I do not have the same reaction I did towards him the first time. Maybe I will get lucky and he has grown horns and a hairy hoof since last week. However, the moment he comes through the door, my heart rises in my chest, settling in my throat.

There are no horns or a hoof.

Fudge. I am in trouble.

Jonah has a deep bruising on the right side of his face and a small cut on his lip. Even when marred, he is still beautiful. His green eyes are all over me as I break character and ask, "What happened? How did you get those bruises?"

He tilts his head and gives me a "why do you care?" face and I immediately change the subject; grateful I have not turned on the tape recorder for this interview just yet.

Placing my hand on the recorder, I prepare him, "Okay Jonah, are you ready? Are you comfortable talking to me today? Last time you did not say much, we need more than one-word answers if this is going to be helpful to the research."

He takes an eternity to respond, "I can do that . . . Sarah." He drags Sarah out slowly, exaggerating his southern drawl, hinting his doubt at this being my real name. Ignoring the indication, I switch the recorder on.

"So, you want to know about my bruises?" His right eyebrow raises quizzically.

"If you want to share that, you can."

"I got punched. This is prison, people get punched all the time. What else do you want to know?" He is being a smart-ass and I don't appreciate it.

"Anything you want to tell me," I respond, prompting him with some of the interview questions, "what was it like growing up? Where are you from and what were your parents like?"

After a couple of seconds, I am surprised to get an answer.

"I grew up in Georgia with my mom. She was a drug addict. She died when I was fourteen of an overdose. I had no family in Georgia, so I got on a bus and headed to my aunt's house in Virginia. She didn't want me though because she had kids of her own and really couldn't take care of me, so I went into foster care for a while. I never knew who my father was. My mother would work the streets for money, for drugs, so I doubt she even knew who he was."

I do not want him to stop talking, so I remain quiet hoping he will elaborate, and much to my shock he does, "It was hard, I ended up in some scary foster homes. I decided when I was sixteen that I needed out of the system, so I ran away. I began stealing so that I could survive on the streets."

Finally, we are getting somewhere.

I prompt him again, "That sounds very difficult Jonah, where did you sleep?"

"Under a bridge in a quiet part of town. By this time, I was living in Baltimore. I would dig through trash trying to find food. I had a friend of mine named Ezekiel who was homeless like me, so we stuck together. We did what we had to, so that we could get by. I was never proud to steal but I had no choice."

"What about school?" I say, already presuming to know the answer.

"I dropped out as soon as I left the foster home."

"Did you become an addict?" I ask this knowing that this is a common occurrence for individuals who come from these types of situations, even thinking he probably sold drugs as well to support himself.

He pauses and thinks for a moment, "I was never an addict. I would smoke weed but that was it. I was never interested in the hard stuff because I saw what it did to my mom."

He makes direct eye contact and I know he is being honest. The slight downturn of the corner of his eyebrows only heightening his sadness at this truth.

We continue the conversation by discussing the violent acts he committed as a youth. He explains that he would get into fights, "I think I fought a lot because I was so angry. I felt that the world was so unfair. I didn't understand why I had to be born into such a crappy situation. Why I never had a normal home like other people. Now, after spending a few years behind bars, I have learned a lesson."

"What's that?" I ask, genuinely interested.

He looks into my eyes with sudden seriousness and a clenched jaw, "I may have had it rough as a kid, but it could always be worse. At least I was free. Now, all I crave is freedom. Hell, I would love to sleep under a bridge, as long as I wasn't locked up anymore."

His eyebrows furrow together along a crease in his forehead, he rubs his hands together, chains clanking. I have a sudden and overwhelming urge to reach over and touch him, to provide him with some comfort. This urge disturbs me to my very core and is something that I will need to reflect upon later. We finish our conversation with me thanking Jonah for opening up, explaining that he is providing me with the kind of feedback that I need.

He seems pleased and says, "I'm glad my story is good for something."

Jonah stands up to leave, but before he does, he says with a slightly lopsided grin, "Does that mean I will see you next week?"

I respond with a polite nod, which prompts a big, genuine smile from him. It is unexpected, sending a shiver up my spine, not the cold kind but the electric kind. After a pause to remind myself to breathe, I smile back at him. I do it without realizing it and then instantly regret it. The look on his face is a satisfied one; he knows he has an impact on me.

Crap, I am starting to lose my grip. I think this just as an odd sound comes from my throat. Did I just giggle?

Oh my gosh, I cannot be swooning over the smile of a research subject and giggling like a schoolgirl. As he walks out, leaving me, I am left in contemplation; the sound of his footsteps reverberating in my ear. I relax my head and rub my temples with the tips of my fingers in a desperate attempt to make this reaction go away.

I blast the radio and white knuckle the entire drive home, truly perplexed by my response to this man.

Chapter Seven

The entire next day, an undercurrent of uncertainty runs through my subconscious. It is as though a gray river is flowing around me, never leaving my side; taunting me, and reminding me that I am not myself.

I try to focus on work, but it is difficult. I have my headset on and am diligently transcribing the interviews from the day before. When I get to Jonah, I listen to his deep voice while his mischievous smile haunts me. About an hour into the transcription, I tear the headphones off and throw them down on my desk. Luckily, no one notices and the only sound in the room is the quiet flurry of fingers vibrating across keyboards, reminding me of the sound of locusts fluttering their wings; taking me back to summer nights as a child.

A face peers into the room through the small window in the door; startling me until I recognize it is Barry Schmidt, a detective with the F.B.I. He is waving at me to come over, so I get up and leave the room to speak to him in the hallway.

"Hello Detective Schmidt, what can I do for you?"

"Please, call me Barry. I want to take you out for

dinner tonight Madeline. What do you say, you meet me at the Velvet Corner at seven?"

The look on his face is smug, as though he is congratulating himself even before I give him an answer.

Ugh, fine. "Sure, Barry. That would be nice. I'll see you then."

I have not been on a single date since my divorce and I am not even sure I know how to date anymore. He nods with shoulders held high and chest expanded like a peacock. He turns and walks down the hallway; his unremarkable backside and short neck not eliciting any kind of sexual arousal from me but does remind me of a turtle.

All well, maybe it will work out. I do need to be remarried soon so that I can start working on completing the *'having two children by the time I am thirty-seven'* goal so I had better not waste any potential suitors. I am running out of time to be picky.

~~~

That night, Barry meets me at the Velvet Corner, a fantastic restaurant with an even better wine menu. We drink Merlot while dining on plates of Spaghetti Carbonara. The pasta and wine fill my belly as Barry drains my patience.

Barry is the type of person who only wants to have a conversation if it about himself. He supports this thesis by droning on and on about his job, never once asking me anything about myself. As he talks, I notice that he is average. Average height, average weight, average face, average personality. As the evening wears on, I begin to have an aversion to everything about him from the way he speaks to even the way he eats. I watch intently as a piece of basil drifts across the front of his upper teeth, finally wedging itself in between two incisors. The basil stares at me for most of the night and I begin to feel it is mocking me.

This disappointing date makes me wonder, why did I agree to this? Am I bored? Is that why I am finding myself attracted to a dangerous convict? I know I want passion, but what is passion really? Is danger the same as passion? I have never really experienced anything truly exciting and I certainly have never done anything remotely controversial or spontaneous. Maybe Min was right and that is what my problem is.

As I consider seeing my therapist again, Barry suggests we head back to my place for a nightcap,

"Listen, how 'bout we head back to your place for a drink. I don't want this evening to end."

Frustrated with my lack of rebelliousness, I go against my better judgment and agree, hoping the basil works its way out of his teeth before his mouth touches mine.

~~~

Back at my place, and under the spell that only a glass of good wine can cast, I surprise even myself and end up having sex with Barry.

If you can call it that.

Bland Barry continues to disappoint by tearing the clothes off his turtle-like body and crawling all over me. After a few quick pumps, he is done, and I am left wishing I could turn back time.

I have not slept with anyone since my husband so this should be a big deal for me. I was never promiscuous in my twenties and my ex-husband was only the third man I had ever had sex with. Instead of it being a big deal, I store it in the back of my head, vowing to forget it ever happened.

Afterward, when I notice he is not anxious to leave my apartment, I encourage him to go home, "Barry, I need to get up early for a meeting tomorrow. Do you mind calling it a night?"

He seems shocked by my request and quips, "You don't have to say that I'll stay. I know how you women are."

Still not getting the hint, I say flatly, "No really, it would be best if you left."

Grateful when he finally leaves, I shower then lay in bed with earbuds in, listening to Lord Huron's "The Night We Met" pondering if I should burn the sheets or not.

The lyrics "and then I can tell myself, what the hell I'm supposed to do, and then I can tell myself, not to ride along with you," pulse in my ears.

What is hell is going on with me?

Chapter Eight

It is two days before our next session at the prison and Dr. Flanigan is choosing the four inmates that will participate in the extended interviews. She makes us wait until it is the end of the workday and as we are packing up our things, she comes out of her office to tell us whom she has chosen. Similar to an episode of the Bachelor, we are all anxious to hear which inmates will get the final rose, and I am panicking that she will choose Jonah.

My worst fear is confirmed as she hands the rose over, "Maddie, I want you to keep working with inmate Jonah M. I know we had concerns about him after the first interview, but he opened up during the last one. I also felt that he was the most honest of the three. What do you think?"

Bloody hell.

"Um . . . well . . . I think they each offer something very different. Freddy discussed his gang affiliation and I seemed to hit a nerve with Tyson about his childhood. Jonah did open up the most in the second interview though. I could see working with any of them."

"Great, it is settled then, go ahead with inmate Jonah

M."

"Will do Dr. Flanigan."

Balls.

This is bad. I am holding my breath all the way to the parking lot, passing by a dozen other F.B.I. employees, not listening to the murmurs about a storm coming in tonight. I do not care about a storm as I have to get home and try to figure out how to approach this research, how to stop this attraction. I notice a slight dull throbbing in my temple, and I rub it while dialing my therapist to schedule an appointment. She is out of office, so I leave a voicemail. My determination to remain professional with Jonah overwhelms my thoughts on the drive home, distracting me from the obvious dark storm clouds that are building along the horizon.

~~~

Late that evening, as I lounge on my bed eating leftover Chang's, I try to force myself to relax by reading a book. I was going to go for a love story but, thought better of it and picked up a murder mystery instead.

Two pages in, I give up, throw the book down, letting out an exasperated sigh. My stomach is in knots and what started as a dull headache, is now, decidedly not dull. As

I search for some Aspirin, a shadow darts across the wall, drawing my attention towards the window. Several dark figures are streaming in, skipping across my bedroom floor.

Oh *yeah,* there was something about a storm coming.

I slide out of my bed and look out the window, opening it slightly. The wind has picked up and the usually busy street below is empty creating a post-apocalyptic scene. A single plastic shopping bag that whips up from the ground, turning rapidly, eventually, lodging itself in the tree outside my window, struggling to escape. In spring, the tree is bright with small pink flower blossoms but now it has leafless branches that are severe as they reach up towards the sky.

Thunder erupts, the loud rumbling jolting me back from the window.

I sprint through my apartment and make sure all the windows are shut.

Once satisfied, I turn to the weather channel so that weatherman Eric can warn me how bad it is going to get.

"This is going to be a big one, get ready for a long night everyone as it is going to be hard to sleep with the sound of thunder erupting for the next several hours."

Just *great.*

Chapter Nine

The ferocious storm rages on through the night; I lay in bed wrapped in my comforter wishing I were not alone. The heavy rain causes substantial damage throughout the city, earning the title of *The Storm of the Century*. My apartment building loses power for three days; many of the buildings downtown damaged, with some destroyed.

The F.B.I. headquarters is sturdy though and manages to escape unscathed much to Dave's dismay the next morning at work, "Man, I could have used a few days off work. I haven't taken a vacation in years. But no, of course, this building is completely fine."

Dave flicks the end of his cigarette, ash falling onto the wet cement.

"Ya know, most people would be happy a building didn't get destroyed in a storm Dave," says Henry sarcastically as he shakes his head.

"Yeah, yeah. Maddie, wouldn't you have liked a vacation? I don't think you've ever even taken a day off. Lord knows you could use it."

"What's that supposed to mean, Dave?"

Glancing toward Henry with an "I've said too much" face, he tries to recover, "I just mean that you work hard Maddie, and everyone needs a break every once in a while. Don't get your panties in a bunch."

With that, I head back inside. What the hell did he mean by that? Do I need a vacation?

~~~

Over the next few days, I stew over Dave's comment as we work on finishing transcribing and fine-tuning our research plan. Only one time does Boring Barry stop by and attempt to speak with me. When he waves through the window, I pretend not to see him. Luckily, he takes the hint and does not come again so I can continue pretending that it never happened.

The North Branch Correctional Institution did not fare as lucky as the F.B.I. headquarters in the storm. We cannot conduct our research with the inmates this week because the prison needs time to repair the damage, they do not want us there due to safety concerns and limited staffing.

Grateful to have a break from meeting with the inmates, I use this time to gather myself and arrange to start seeing my therapist again next week. I went to her briefly after my mother died and again after my divorce but stopped because I felt that I could take care of myself without help.

Apparently, I was wrong.

Chapter Ten

Before I know it, a week has gone by and I find myself sitting across the metal table from Jonah again. My heartbeat quickens every time I see him, which is extremely annoying, and for some inexplicable reason, he also fills me with so much anxiety that I fidget and sweat through my clothes. The barbaric nature my body has in response to him is off-putting. Nobody has ever made me sweat, other than my aerobics instructor. My first therapy session is tomorrow, and maybe Dr. Abby can sort this out for me.

Before we start recording, Jonah slides a small piece of paper to me. I hesitate but take the paper even though I know I should not.

"What is this?"

"Read it. Please."

I slowly open the small, stained, lined notebook paper.

I missed you last week.

Crap.

What do I do now?

"Jonah, I don't know what to say. You can't do this. I could lose my job if I were anything but professional with you. Do you understand?" My shaking hand betrays the professional image I am desperate to portray.

"I understand. I just wanted you to know since this is our last meeting. Forgive me?" After he says this, he bites his lower lip slightly and I think I might die.

With a face like that, how could I not forgive him?

"Yes. I forgive you, and I was going to ask you about that. We have decided we need to get some more information from you, that three one-hour long meetings were not enough. I would like to meet with you two more times, for two hours at a time if you're willing, but if we do, you can't cross any more boundaries with me."

Jonah does not respond but looks at me with eyes wide with surprise.

"Well, what do you think Jonah?"

He looks down at his hands and I can tell he is thinking. His lips purse in a straight line before he bites down again at the bottom corner of his mouth; he takes his time before answering, torturing me.

My heart is beating so fast it hurts. I feel faint. It dawns on me, what if he says no? The thought of never seeing him again is almost unbearable.

After what seems like an eternity, he looks up and says

so quietly I almost don't hear him, "I should probably say no, but I don't think I can . . . I will do it."

After a pause, I ask with trepidation, "Why should you say no, Jonah?"

He sighs, "You need to know, Sarah, that I am not really a violent person. I mean, I'm a thief but I'm not violent. Maybe you should pick someone else for your research."

Stunned, I urge him to elaborate, "What do you mean by that Jonah?"

"Look, I've been in fights as a kid growing up, but that's the extent of it. I only robbed homes when I knew the people wouldn't be there. I would stake out a place and wait until it was empty before the hit. I never wanted to hurt anybody." His face has a look that I can only describe as pain, mixed with another undetectable emotion.

"What about the crime that got you sent here? It says in your file that you were convicted of robbery and assault with a deadly weapon."

Forcefully, he quickly responds, "I know what it says. I know what I'm here for, but what you don't understand is that I didn't think they were home. Zeek told me he had been watching the house and he knew it was empty. I didn't know until it was too late that he had lied because he knew I wouldn't help him with the hit if the owners were home. He is the one who beat them. I didn't. Instead, I ran. I never put a finger on them. When we went to trial, the cops said that both Zeek and l physically assaulted the homeowners and we both got convicted for it. They lied and now my case is up for retrial because of it. I'm not a violent person, but I've made mistakes and I'm not a good guy, but just so you know, I'm not the same man that I once was. I've changed. I know that violence is what this research is about because that's what I was told when I was asked to participate. I shouldn't have agreed to this project at all. I'm sorry."

The revelation sends chills down my spine. Somehow, I know when I look into his eyes that he is telling the truth, however, it is a declaration that I am unprepared for.

"Why didn't you tell me? Why did you agree to this project?" I blurt out, not even trying to sound composed.

"I dunno, I just wanted to talk to someone new for a change. I'm tired of talking to criminals and the guards. Then, after that first day and I saw you, I didn't want the conversations to end. I wanted to keep seeing you. Seeing you is the only good thing in my life." Jonah says this without hesitation, but quickly appears nervous, his jaw tensing as his hair falls into his eyes.

"Your case is up for retrial?"

"Yeah. It was scheduled for March but has been postponed for October. Mark Wessley, my lawyer, is pushing to have the assault charge dropped."

"So, you could be a free man?"

"I doubt it, I will still probably be locked up for years. I don't want to get my hopes up too much."

"Okay, Jonah. Thanks for telling me. I will check with my supervisor after our session today and see if she wants me to continue the research with someone else. Let's get through today first." Buying time and not wanting to end the session, I switch the tape recorder on, unsure about what to do next.

My, "you can do this," mantra rattles around my skull as I try to build up the nerve to stay instead of run. My instinct is screaming at me to leave, threatening my very sense of safety if I stay sitting across from this man.

In a moment of horror, I realize I muttered this mantra.

"What Sarah? I heard you say, 'you can do this'?

What can you do?"

I switch the recorder back off, "I didn't mean to say that out loud. I was trying to give myself a pep talk."

"What kind of pep talk? Are you nervous to be around me?" With a dear in caught in headlights look, I say nothing.

"Are you afraid of me?" His voice strains as if the words are inflicting pain.

My mouth is agape as I try to come up with an answer.

Sounding pathetic, I mutter, "Um, I don't know why I said that Jonah. I didn't mean for you to hear that. I guess I am afraid of you in a way. But not the way you think I am."

I *cannot* believe I just said that.

"Then how? How're you afraid of me?" I don't answer. "Sarah, are you attracted to me? I'm getting a vibe that you are, but I have been locked up for a long time, my ability to read women is probably way off."

Oh. My. Gosh.

"I ask because if that is the case, I want you to know that I won't do anything to make you uncomfortable even though I am very attracted to you as well; I will keep my hands to myself. I don't really have a choice in here," he raises his cuffed hands as he says this; "I could still do this project with you without it being a problem, if that is what you want. But please, don't be afraid of me, I'd never hurt you."

I take a long, deep breath, "Okay Jonah. It's truth time. Yes, I'm attracted to you, but I really cannot even discuss it. It has to end with this conversation. Let's get back to the research for now, okay?"

Jonah's green eyes are wide, he blinks rapidly and says, "Okay," I reach over to turn on the tape recorder, "but only if you tell me your real name."

He lifts one brow in a cocky manner as he says this. I do not want to lie to him.

"My name is Madeline. Maddie for short."

"I like that name."

I blush immediately and I know it. When I look up, I see that he is blushing too. I turn the recorder is on, getting back to business, doing everything I can to keep it together and to not be drawn in by that face and those eyes.

Disappointedly, I fail miserably and end up noticing for the first time a light dusting of freckles around his nose. It is almost more than I can handle.

Chapter Eleven

As soon as I am home after the session with inmate Jonah, I pace around my apartment. I am treading a thin line here. *I have to snap out of this.* I pull the crinkled note he wrote me out of my coat jacket and hold it over the trash can in the kitchen. I drop the piece of paper and watch as it floats in the air and lands on the banana peel from this morning. I nod as if to say, "good job," like this simple gesture will solve all the world's problems.

I congratulate myself too soon because, much to my horror, that night I dream of flecks of gold while the words *I missed you* ripple through my subconscious, threatening to tear down the walls of protection I have so diligently built. Like a storm brewing, I can feel the pressure mounting, indicating something is coming.

~~~

After an uneventful day at work, I leave early to meet with Dr. Abby. With last night's dream still vivid, I am eager to speak to her.

Dr. Abby opens her office door, the large bangle jewelry on her wrist clanking as she does, taking me back to the times I have been here before.

"Madeline, hello. It's so great to see you, dear. Please come in." Lavender wafts past me when I enter her domain, instantly calming me down.

"How have you been, it's been around five months since I saw you last, right? I've been thinking about you, hoping things are well."

"Well, I'm here, so things must not be going well at all Dr. Abby," I lean back on the comfortable blue sofa, ready to let it all out.

"I see. Go ahead and tell me what's been going on."

I jump right in and tell her about the research project and the problem of my attraction to my research subject, "He's good looking and yesterday he wrote me a note saying that he missed me last week and told me he was attracted to me and asked me if I was to him. Then last night, I threw the note he wrote away, but it didn't help because I dreamed about him all night."

"And? What did you say, Maddie?" Her salt and pepper hair comforting me with its wisdom; encouraging me to be honest.

"Say to what?"

"You just said he asked you if you were attracted to him. What did you say when he asked you this?"

"Oh, that. I told him that I was."

Dr. Abby leans her head to the side like a puppy does when trying to understand what you are saying.

"It's okay though, Dr. Abby, because I told him that this has to remain professional if we are going to continue this project."

"Don't you think you already destroyed that by stating that you were also attracted to him?"

Crap-on-a-cracker.

"Don't answer that Madeline, you already know the answer. Have you thought about talking with your supervisor about this? I think you have an ethical obligation to do so. You're risking that the research you are conducting, will be biased. Of course, you are also risking your job."

"I know Dr. Abby. I haven't talked to her about it yet, but I need to, but I don't want her to lose respect for me. I'll never get that promotion if she knows about this. Also, there's more…He told me that he is not the type of offender we are trying to research. You see, we are looking to interview dangerous, violent criminals. He was convicted for robbery and assault with a deadly weapon, but he stated he never actually assaulted anybody. His case is up for retrial because the police lied in their testimony," words are pouring out of my mouth like a tap with no nozzle.

"Maddie, that's all the more reason that you need to go to your supervisor. If you don't then you are making the conscious decision to continue this research with him even though you know you should pull out."

"I know."

"What are you going to do?"

"I don't know . . . I mean, of course, I know. I'll talk to my supervisor on Monday. I have to. What I really need your help with though is helping me get over this attraction. I don't want to react to him this way anymore."

"Well, that's tough Maddie, but if you stop working with him and remove him completely from your life then that will help."

"Yes, but why is this happening? How could I be attracted to him? I don't understand it."

"Hmm, well, perhaps you are just experiencing what we 'shrinks' like to call displaced emotions. These occur when a person subconsciously redirects from the true object to a safer one. Inmate Jonah is a safer option because he is not a real threat. He is behind bars, thereby eliminating the possibility of a true romantic relationship. The real issue is that you are lonely and still recovering from your divorce. Do not be so hard on yourself about the attraction and, instead, work through the real emotions, the real issues. If you keep coming to see me, I can help you with that."

"Displaced emotions? Okay, I can live with that. Thanks, Dr. I will come back next week."

I appreciate her advice but do not feel any less tense as I leave her office.

Chapter Twelve

The next few days are, by all accounts, normal. I do all of my normal activities, eat all of my normal foods, sleep, and work. However, something is off. Stress flowing through me, just under the top layer of my skin, and is distracting my every thought, building pressure with each passing moment. I spend days questioning my own sanity. I go back and forth on whether or not I should confide in Dr. Flanigan. A part of me is afraid of the judgment she will pass onto me; another, deeper part of me does not want to stop seeing Jonah. However, while I am worried about what Dr. Flanigan would think of me, no one is judging me more than myself.

When the fourth session with inmate Jonah arrives, he is clearly surprised to see me; his eyes are as big as saucers as he says, "Maddie? I'm so glad to see you. I was worried that last week was going to be the last time."

I resort to lying, "Hello Jonah, I spoke to my boss and she said to continue working with you. She did not want to waste the work we have already done, so here I am."

The look on his face is one of doubt and I know he recognizes the lie; I just hope he does not call me on it.

"Okay, great Maddie. I mean Sarah. I'm glad to see you but don't worry, I won't say anything with that thing recording that I shouldn't." A small, knowing smile creeps across his face and I should be irritated by his cockiness but instead I smile back.

Jonah is the most open he has been, he answers all of my questions and even elaborates without prompts. It seems that he wants to share. He smiles more but only when he mentions his friend Ezekiel. He explains Zeek is serving an even longer sentence but in a different prison.

I study his face, his body language. I know it seems unlikely, but he appears gentle to me. He does not have the mannerisms of someone who would want to hurt anybody. As these observations come to mind, I check myself because I recognize this has potential bias that I am worried about. Perhaps my attraction to him is causing me to see him how I want to see him, not how he is.

I also find myself enjoying listening to the way he speaks. Not just his deep, soft, southern voice but also the way in which he speaks. He seems very self-aware. It is refreshing in a way to listen to someone speak so honestly. Most people I know lie to themselves all the time. Jonah does not do this. He tells me his flaws. He knows his mistakes. In a way, he has an emotional intelligence I was not expecting.

After I shut the recording off at the end of the session, he takes the opportunity to say that he wishes he could learn more about me, "I wish that I could listen to you talk for two hours instead of you sitting here listening to me. I want to know everything about you, Maddie."

"Jonah, I told you, you can't say stuff like that to me." Please. Do not. I cannot handle it.

"I know, but at least I waited until the recorder was turned off so nobody will know. I can't help but be a little naughty."

My throat catches, as I know this is dangerous, the flirting. I hold my mouth shut tight and stare down at my notepad, stopping myself from saying anything I will regret.

He quickly gathers himself and drawls, "Sorry, I know that I should not have said that. I didn't mean anything by it. I just don't get to speak to many people outside of these walls so when I get a chance to, I'm eager to learn about them."

I look up at him; his eyes lighting up and he smiles

wide, and my gosh, it is brilliant, and I could swear time stands still as I smile back at him. He leans back in the chair, the two front legs lifting off the ground. He is relaxed and pushes the sleeves of his orange prison uniform up his forearms. I need to get out of here, I should not be here, but something catches my eye. A small black tattoo on his wrist consisting of three lines and four dots. An excuse to extend our meeting presents itself so I jump on it.

"This is not part of the research but out of curiosity, what does the tattoo on your wrist mean?" Jonah looks down at his arm pulling up his shirtsleeve to give me a better look.

"It's kind of dorky so don't laugh," he says this with a lopsided grin that is almost unbearable, "it's a symbol meaning thief. I saw it in the movie The Hobbit. Gandalf scratched it onto Bilbo's door so that the dwarves could find his house."

"Oh, I see. What made you get that done?"

Jonah blinks his long lashes as he explains, "Well, it fits me. That's what I am. A thief. It reminds me of who I am so it will keep me in my place."

"That is not all you are Jonah," I say this without even

thinking.

"That's nice of you to say, but I'm not so sure it is true. I'm a changed man, I don't want to ever steal anything again, but I'm not sure there is much more to me."

Instinctually, I reach out and slowly run my index finger across his wrist; lingering as I get to the small tattoo; feeling the warmth of Jonah's skin while admiring the blue veins running up his forearm into the palm of his large hands.

His eyes are all over me and his is jaw clenched; I immediately know I went too far and abruptly remove my finger.

"I'm so sorry Jonah," the words barely a whisper.

"I'm not."

Jonah puts his hand into his pocket and pulls out a small piece of paper, wordlessly sliding it across to me. It reads; *Can I write to you after this is over?*

I fumble for my pen and quickly jot down: *I can't.*

Jonah takes my pen and writes; *I understand. I had to take my shot. Only those who dare to fail miserably can achieve greatly.*

I need to leave this room.

There is so much tension in here, I worry the guard can feel it too; the oppression filling the space in the room, exuding from every pore on our bodies.

Jonah uses this opportunity to talk about what he enjoys; trying to keep the conversation going so that I do not leave, "I love to read, and I write sometimes."

"Really? What do you write?"

"Just little, short stories," he goes on and asks me, "if I gave you a short story that I wrote, would you read and let me know what you think of it?"

I shrug, "Okay Jonah."

"Thanks, I brought it with me just in case." Out of his back pocket, he pulls out the story, handing it to me as the chains on his wrists rattle.

I quickly stick the story into my briefcase and stand up to leave. I cannot find any more reasonable reasons for staying here, "I'll see you next week Jonah," I say as I rush out of the room.

"Bye Maddie."

After I get into my car, I grab the phone and look up the quote. To my surprise, John F. Kennedy said it. I have a twenty-six-year-old, high school dropout, convicted criminal, and self-proclaimed thief quoting JFK to me.

Whatever I thought I knew about Jonah, or criminals in general, I am learning I was wrong. I pride myself on being able to read a person's personality, on being able to understand the type of person who commits crimes. I always believed criminals were just people who made bad decisions because they come from bad childhoods or are mentally ill. Disturbed by the possibility that I still have a lot to learn, and that maybe, just maybe, criminals, and even myself, are not as straightforward as we seem.

~~~

I walk through my front door; drop all of my stuff on the floor, fall onto the couch to read the story Jonah gave me. It is handwritten on beat up, stained notepad paper. As I run my finger over the now familiar handwriting, I think of the touch of Jonah's skin. The residual sensation of his warmth on my fingertip leaks onto the pages in front of me; radiating the words inked across the page.

Melting into the couch, I allow Jonah's words to surround me.

He writes about a boy. A boy who gains the ability to become invisible whenever he wants. The boy starts by using the ability only occasionally to spy on neighbors, girls in locker rooms, and to escape the hard times, like when his parents would fight. This switch to invisibility progresses from, an occasional escape, to the boy remaining invisible most of the time. He learns that it is easier to be nothing rather than to be something. Then one night as he watches his family laughing and eating dinner, he becomes sad. He wants to turn back to visible again so that he can share in their laughter, however, when he tries to be visible again, he is not able to. In despair, he spends the rest of his life invisible, desperately regretting his decision, watching the world pass him by until one day he can no longer take it anymore and ends his life by jumping from a cliff into the sea below.

I grip the story in my hands; tears streaming from my eyes and falling onto the words below, staining the pages.

Chapter Thirteen

I hurry to see Dr. Abby Friday afternoon, eager to tell someone about the session with Jonah.

My face must be displaying my emotions because, the moment Dr. Abby sees me, she says, "Oh my Maddie, sit down and tell me what happened."

"I'm confused, Dr. Abby. It must be something with me, maybe my divorce, maybe loneliness. Maybe that displaced emotions thing, maybe all of the above."

She hesitates before asking, "Maddie, what happened?"

"I touched him. I touched his arm and lingered, flirted. I know an arm touch should not be a big deal, and in normal circumstances, it wouldn't be, but that was so inappropriate. I could lose my job for doing something like that."

"Maddie, I'm going to ask you a tough question, what do you think your life is missing? What are you seeking from this crush?"

"A crush? I don't have a crush on him no. NO. There is no way Dr. Abby. I would never have a crush on someone like him. I am just attracted to him, and I dunno

. . . lonely or something. I thought you said this was just displaced emotions?" I spit this out a bit too forcefully.

Dr. Abby looks at me with a slight arch in her brow, "Yes, I did say that, and it may be, but I think we need to dive deeper into why this attraction, as you call, it has evolved to the point that you are risking your employment and that is significant. Also Maddie, what do you mean by someone like him?"

"Oh, you know what I mean Dr. Abby, someone like him, a criminal."

She nods and says, "I see Maddie, we will talk more about that later. For today, I want to talk about why this is happening. Why are you allowing yourself to cross these ethical boundaries? What is it that you are seeking?"

I thought she was supposed to tell me that.

"I don't know Dr. I have never felt like this before."

"Like what Maddie?"

"Lost . . . I have never felt so lost. I have never felt this way other than when my mother died. I have always been so certain of everything. Now I don't feel like I am sure about anything."

"Maddie, I believe that you are in the throes of a life crisis. You are at a crossroads in your life and you need to either learn from it, or you can run from it and remain feeling this way indefinitely."

"Like a midlife crisis? Dr. Abby, I'm only thirty-two."

A soft, patient smile falls on her lips, immediately comforting me, "I know Maddie, but you can have a life crisis really at any age. It's not uncommon for someone to hit thirty or to have gone through a divorce to experience the growing pains you are now. Also, and please listen to me without getting defensive if you can, this behavior is selfish of you. You're risking a large research project including the work of others."

"I know. And I know you're right. How do I make it stop Dr. Abby?"

"Introspection. Try to uncover why you are going through this. What is it that you are trying to tell yourself? What are you seeking? Here is what we know, you are unhappy, you feel lost, you are dissatisfied with the status quo of your life. You want to change but you are unsure of what to change. I have a suggestion, but you are not going to like it, Maddie. I suggest that you try to embrace whatever it is you want to do and see where it takes you. Instead of forcing your life in a certain direction, try to go with the flow, accept the things you cannot control, and embrace it for what it is. Messy and unpredictable."

"That sounds horrible."

A quick laugh from Dr. Abby leads me to laugh too, "Maddie, I know it is for someone like you, someone who tries to live by a life plan. Try with small things first, say yes, instead of no. Be more spontaneous. Hell, have some fun."

Fun? Spontaneous? First Min and now my shrink? Either both these women have no common sense, or I am missing something.

"Okay, Dr. Abby. Maybe I will . . . Actually, I did the other night; I slept with someone I barely know, the first person since my divorce. Can you believe that? It was terrible too. Definitely not fun but it was spontaneous."

"It may not have been sexually satisfying but I am glad you are trying things that are out of your comfort zone. I encourage you to keep doing that."

"Are you saying that I should keep interacting with Jonah the way that I am?"

"Oh, heavens no Maddie. You should live a little, but not at the cost of your job. I assume you have not spoken with your boss about any of this have you?" Her inflection betraying her nonjudgmental demeanor.

I opt for lies, "No, I did Dr. Abby. I didn't mention that I was attracted to him, but I did tell her that he claims not to be violent, but she wants me to keep working with him." I cannot believe I am lying to my shrink.

"Okay, Maddie. Let's talk more about that next time."

I leave Dr. Abby's office without mentioning Jonah's short story or the way it made me cry. I want to protect it, protect the invisible boy somehow.

Chapter Fourteen

It is Saturday and I need something to keep my mind off Jonah, so I invite Min over. She brings with her a bottle of Moscato and a trusty bag of Cheetos, our favorites, and dives in before I can even take my first bite.

"Well? What's going on? You rarely ask me to hang out randomly and you never want me to come over here, so something is up. What is it?"

Darn, she knows me too well.

"I want to tell you something, but I ask first that you withhold judgment."

"Oh, this is going to be good. Spill it." Her dark brown eyes spark thanks to the promise of something titillating.

"First, you don't have to even suggest it because I've already started seeing Dr. Abby again."

"Oh man, don't keep me in suspense. Get to it girl."

A deep sigh and I dive in, "Well, I told Jonah I was attracted to him, and I touched him. Nothing major Min, I just ran my finger over the tattoo on his wrist, and"

"Wait for just one second Maddie. Jonah? Are you talking about that hot inmate you are working with? You told him you are attracted to him and you TOUCHED him?!"

"Yes, I know. It gets worse. He told me that he was not the type of offender we thought he was, and I've failed to mention any of this to my boss."

"Why haven't you told your boss? Isn't that an ethical problem for your research? I'm sure you could get fired for something like this Maddie."

"Oh yeah, big time, and I don't know. I think it's because she would want me to continue the work with a different inmate and I don't want to stop seeing him."

"So, hold up. Let me get this straight. Madeline Tilltot, perfect Madeline, rule-abiding, never-does-anything-impractical Madeline, has intentionally chosen to do something wrong? I'm shocked, flummoxed. This is so unlike you; I feel like I don't even know you."

This, I was not expecting, "What do you mean?"

"Look, don't get me wrong, I'm your best friend. I'll always love you, but this is crazy Maddie. What has gotten into you? You could lose everything and for what? You can't get anything from this. He can't even be in a relationship. He is locked up for years!" Min is growing anxious.

"I know I know. You are right. I don't know what I'm doing Min."

"You know, this is the first time you have ever done anything wrong in your life. This is the first time you have ever acted like a human."

"What? You don't think I act like a human?"

"You have never made a bad decision. Not once. You never once stayed out too late, never once slept with the wrong guy, never once missed class, or cheated on a test or anything. I love you girl but that is some hard stuff to live up to."

Processing what she is saying, I opt for more wine while she continues, "Maddie, this is heavy. I want you to know that I love you so don't take offense to any of this, but please hear me out."

"Okay, I'm trying Min."

Min takes a minute before going on, "Maddie, I've been having some issues lately in my marriage. I have not been handling them well and Raymond thinks I have a drinking problem. I didn't want to tell you because you're always so black and white; I thought it'd be hard to talk to you about it truthfully. I didn't think you would be very understanding."

Experiencing a genuine feeling of shock and regret, I immediately reply, "Min, I'm sorry that I'm not easier to talk to. I know I can be rigid. I want you to know that I love you and I support you. Please let me know if there is anything I can do. I'm so sorry I haven't been a friend in the way you need me to be."

"Thank you for saying that Maddie. I appreciate that. I'm just happy to know that you are not perfect, and I can talk to you about these things. But in all seriousness, I'm really worried about you. I'm glad you are seeing Dr. Abby again, but I just hope it is not too late."

"Too late?"

"Yeah, I mean before you lose your job."

"I hope so too, but back to you. What's been going on with you and Raymond?"

"Well, about six months ago I found out he slept with some random chick he met at the gym if you can believe that."

"WHAT?"

"I know, he says it only happened once and he's been saying he is sorry for it ever since. We just started marriage counseling about a month ago. The cheating is not the only problem though; we have not been connecting for a while. He says I've been drinking more than I used to and I don't know. I don't think I have a drinking problem. Of course, I say that with a glass of wine in my hands."

"Let's throw this out Min. We don't need it," I say, holding the bottle of wine in my hands, slightly unbalanced because I have already had one glass too many.

"No, no. We'll finish this for now, but maybe I'll have a dry month. Thanks for letting me talk about this Maddie."

Wow, she does need a friend. I wish I were a better one than what I have been lately.

"So, are we still on for tomorrow night at Mickey's?"

Oh yeah. *That.*

"Sure, I guess so."

Half an hour later, we exchange goodbyes, and she promises to text me when she gets home. Sitting on my new couch with nothing left around me to distract those intrusive thoughts. The familiar ping of loneliness begins to creep in but dissipates when I finally give in and let Jonah drift to the forefront of my mind. I cannot help but feel good thinking about him.

I fantasize about what it would be like to have his lips against mine, his hands stroking the curves of my body. Pressure builds in my abdomen as I picture him taking off his clothes and looking at me darkly underneath his long eyelashes. I imagine him getting on his knees in front of me; pulling my bottom to the edge of the sofa so that he can run his tongue along my hipbone while never breaking eye contact; the gold flecks in his eyes shimmering. My skin prickles on the back of my neck.

A sudden thud snaps me back into reality.

The twenty-somethings next door have arrived home, slamming the door behind them, turning on music loud enough to wake the dead. I shake my head and put my headphones in. Blood Orange's "You're Not Good Enough," pours into my ears and I get up to dance, trying desperately to dance away the desire.

Chapter Fifteen

It is Sunday and it also happens to be my thirty-third birthday. Dave, Henry, Min, and even Tammy are meeting me for drinks at Mickey's to celebrate. Min could tell yesterday that I am not overly excited about celebrating my birthday, so she calls me beforehand to try to get me in the spirit.

"What's wrong Maddie? You don't seem that excited about tonight. It'll be fun, I promise!"

I sigh, "Thirty-three just feels old to me, I keep thinking that I have not even really started living yet," I say as I stare at my reflection in my bedroom mirror, my freckles glaring back at me.

"Oh Maddie, you have so much for someone your age. Think about it, you have been married, have your master's degree, a successful career, you have done more than what most do in an entire lifetime."

My response is sarcastic, "Yeah, and a thirty-three-year-old divorcee who fancies a criminal and lives in a tiny apartment. Sounds highly successful to me!"

"Perk up Maddie and let's have fun tonight."

"Sure, okay. See you soon," I hang up and do my best

to cheer myself up by drinking a glass of wine and listening to my favorite musical artist, Kygo, while getting dressed. The upbeat sound of "Stole the Show" rings in my ears as I look for a birthday outfit that makes me look younger than thirty-three.

"I should've bought something new," I say aloud, scolding myself.

I finally land on a spaghetti strap red dress that sits above me knee, accented with black heels and dangly earrings. It is a sexy look, leaving me momentarily satisfied. A dark voice pushes through my subconscious asking if I think Jonah would like it, but I push it back.

My phone rings again and it is my father. I have not spoken to him in a couple of months, so I had better answer.

"Hello?"

"Hey darlin', how are you? Happy birthday. How old are you now? Sixty-eight?"

"Haha, very funny dad. I'm doing okay, I guess. How are you?"

"Same. Good. I guess."

"Anything new?"

"No, not at all. Just wondering when you are going to

come for a visit."

And there's the guilt. "Sorry dad, I know it has been a while. I'll try to make it back for the fourth of July or something."

"Okay sweetie, I just miss you is all."

"Miss you too; I'll call you later okay?" I say this knowing that I will not.

"Sure, talk to you soon."

"Okay bye."

The conversation may seem abrupt, but this is how we always are. At least how we have been since mom died. I love my father very much, but I was a mother's girl for sure and once we lost her, we never could figure out how to connect.

I finish getting ready and take one last look in the mirror. I shrug at my reflection; it will have to do.

~~~

Walking through the front door of Mickey's, everyone bellows Happy Birthday. I do what is expected and feign happiness.

Luckily, the night involves dancing, drinking, and plenty of laughs so my unhappiness is temporarily forgotten. After several younger men make passes at me,

I am no longer as down about being thirty-three, of course, that could also be the effects of the alcohol. I notice Min just drinks water and I think that I need to keep an eye on her and be more aware of what is going on with her; my friendship skills have apparently been severely lacking.

As the night ends, people start to drop off. By midnight, it is just Dave and I talking about what it is like to get older.

After a minute, I realize I did not see his wife stop by, so I ask him, "Hey where's your wife tonight?"

Dave seems oddly put off by the question and says, "She wasn't invited."

"What do you mean?" I ask surprised.

"Listen Maddie, my wife and I are separated. I haven't told anyone yet, but I wanted you to know."

Why?

"Oh, I'm so sorry to hear that Dave."

He looks at me surprised and says, "You are?"

The question is odd, maybe I am not noticing social cues thanks to all the alcohol in my system. It might be time to go home.

I grab my purse off the bar counter to leave, but Dave

continues, "Maddie, I think that we can both admit that we are attracted to each other. Now that I'm single, what do you say we give us a shot?"

Completely stunned, I am suddenly very annoyed, "What the hell are you talking about Dave?" Darn, I wish I hadn't had so much to drink tonight; I do not want to overreact but do not seem to have any control over it.

"Come on Maddie; don't deny that we have some major sexual tension going on. I know that you are into me. We don't need to hide it anymore. Know that I am game. Let's do this."

Disappointed in men in general, I respond firmly, "Dave, we're friends and nothing more and now I'm not even sure we are that!"

Dave rolls his eyes, clearly exacerbated.

"So, what, you will screw random detectives but not me? Or is it criminals who you are into now? Am I not dangerous enough for you? Have I not broken enough laws for you to fuck?"

With that revelation, I stand and walk out of the bar to call an Uber.

On the ride home, I am getting angrier and angrier. How does Dave know about stupid boring Barry? Does he know that I am into Jonah? The most important question though is how is it that I keep getting surprised by people? I thought I could read people, I thought I understood their behaviors. I was clearly wrong. Everyone keeps surprising me including myself and it is getting exhausting.

Chapter Sixteen

It is Monday morning at the end of March and the ice is melting, drips of water are tapping against the windowpane. I open my bedroom window and I spot signs of life on the maple tree. Buds of small greenery are running along the branches. The tree appears to be coming to life as the branches gently sway in the breeze; no longer the stark, shadowy figure it was. As I breathe in the fresh spring air, my body feels electrified. Today should be just like any other day. I put my clothes on, have a cup of coffee, brush my teeth, drive to work, and sit down in the same seat, at the same desk I do every day. Only today is not just like any other day.

Today, everything changes.

As I settle at my desk, I hear Dave talking to Henry, and memories from the night before flash in my mind.

"I will just be glad to get through this project. I'm not comfortable being around this individual for extensive periods of time."

Henry nods in agreement, "This is taking a toll on me as well; the offender that I'm working with is the worst type of person to spend time with. I mean he lies, cheats, steals, and has no sense of morality. He does not care for anyone but himself, a true narcissist. I think this will be a common theme for our research and the offender I'm working with certainly demonstrates it," Henry explains, "what's your guy like Tammy?"

"What do you think?" Tammy huffs, "He's disgusting. I'm ready to get through this last meeting. All he does is stare at my chest."

Dave looks at Henry with doubt, "Well these are desperate men."

"What is that supposed to mean Dave?" Tammy bellows.

"That was uncalled for Dave," whoa, did I just stick up for Tammy?

Everyone looks at me with shock, "it's not like you're some prize."

"Whatever Maddie, at least I'm not trying to screw the guy."

"Damn Dave, chill." Henry lifts his hand; indicating Dave has said enough.

Dave and Henry go back to transcribing and Tammy uses her desk chair to roll over to my desk, "Maddie, what did Dave mean by that?"

"He's just being an ass, Tammy. He hit on me last night after everyone left and got mad when I rejected him. Apparently, he's not taking it well."

"Oh, well he's an idiot."

For the first time since she started working here, Tammy smiles at me and I smile back. Maybe I have been too hard on her. Maybe she is just unpleasant because we give her grief all the time.

It is late when Dr. Flanigan arrives, and something is off. She has a whiff of tension on her face, and she is straining a muscle in her neck, as though she is trying to hold back a scream.

As she walks past my desk, she abruptly demands that I come to her office, "Madeline, please come see me at once."

I get up and follow her, leaving my dignity behind.

"Shut the door behind you, Madeline."

I am usually only called Madeline when someone is pissed at me. It is what my ex used to call me during one of our tense non-fight fights. A sinking sensation begins to fill my stomach, forcing me to sit in the chair in front of her desk quickly so that I might not fall over.

"Madeline, I need to talk with you," her accusatory

tone tells me that I am in for it. Does she know about Jonah?

"Okay, what is it, Dr. Flanigan? You seem upset."

She begins, "Why is inmate Jonah M. being included in this project?"

Oh no.

"What do you mean Dr. Flanigan? You chose him as the subject for the extended research."

Annoyed, she nods, "Yes I know that Madeline, but you never told me that he informed you that he wasn't violent. As you well know, we needed to research the most violent offenders. A simple home invasion and robbery was never going to be suitable for the type of research we are trying to conduct."

Fudge nuggets, how does she know?

I lie, "Um, well, I just figured that it was too late to change research subjects." The lies are starting to pile up.

"If I had known that about him, I wouldn't have had you waste your time with him but would've had to finish up the research with one of the other inmates. You should have brought this information to my attention the moment you found out. This was not your decision to make; it was mine as your superior and the leader of this project."

She is visibly disappointed . . . and angry.

"This was a lot of wasted time Maddie, none of the research you did is related to what we are looking at for this project. I will have to throw out all the work you did, or it will be an outlier, skewing the results. What were you thinking with this? I thought you had better judgment than this. More importantly, why didn't you come to me with that information as soon as you had it? Why did I have to hear about it from someone else?"

Shaking, I grip the armrest, my fingers becoming sore. I know that I have screwed up, even more so than what Dr. Flanigan knows.

"I'm sorry Dr. Flanigan. Do you want me to scrap the last session? I don't have a good explanation. I was just interested in his story and I wasn't thinking about the research." What a terrible explanation.

"Uh, Maddie, you weren't thinking about the research? What the hell were you thinking about then? I think this is a bigger issue than you just not finishing the last session."

She pauses before she continues, "There have been rumors that you have developed a crush on this inmate. It has been reported to me, I won't say by who, and it has been noticed by others. So much so, the guard that escorts the inmate has been making jokes about it. Is there any truth to this Madeline? Is that why you continued the research with him without speaking to me about it?"

OH.MY.GOSH.

I knew that I was treading the line, but I had no idea it had become this obvious. My worst fears are coming true and I can feel my feet sinking into the earth below me, threatening to engulf me whole. I have no response. I just look at her, gaping.

She continues, "Look, I spoke to my boss about this situation this morning. He told me that the only thing I can do is to fire you and disregard the work you did."

Stunned, I say, "So that's it? I'm off the team?" My head is spinning.

"Maddie you're a great forensic researcher and for a long time have been my favorite researcher because you always do excellent work. I don't want this to be permanent, but for the time being while I work on smoothing things over, I will have to let you go. I am truly sorry that it has to be this way, but this is a huge lapse in judgment. I don't know if I can trust you anymore."

Oh no. This cannot be happening.

"I'm so sorry Dr. I will gather my things. Please forgive this. I know I messed up, but I hope that the research you have obtained from the others will be enough."

I get up and walk out quickly before I start to cry. Dave, Henry, and Tammy are busy transcribing and do not notice me grab my bag, my few personal items and flee. Tears burst from my eyes the second I pull the car door shut.

Chapter Seventeen

What have I done? How could I do this? How does she know? The only person I told was Min and Dr. Abby. Then, like a pile of bricks falling from the sky, it hits me: last night at my birthday party. I was talking about Jonah with Min. I did not think anyone else overheard me, but they must have.

Maybe Dave.

Racking my brain trying to remember what I said, bits and pieces of the conversation come back to me. She asked me if I told Dr. Flanigan about what Jonah said about not being violent and I vaguely recall saying that I hadn't because I wanted to keep seeing him. That must have been it, my big drunk mouth. If Dave overheard the conversation that would partially explain why he was so weird towards me that night and why he accused me of preferring a criminal to him. He must have come in before I got here this morning and spoke with Dr. Flanigan.

The one thing I did not want to do was to lose my job and here I am. Jobless. I am so disappointed in myself I can barely think straight. I know that the fantasy of mine had to end but why did it have to cost me everything? The right thing to do would be to never speak to Jonah again, drop the entire thing; work on putting my life back together but I cannot do that to him or myself. I want to see him one more time. Hell, I have already lost my job, what is the point of stopping this bad decision train now? The train has already wrecked, so I might as well light it on fire and watch it burn.

Impulsively, I start the car and make the fifty-minute drive to the prison knowing full well that I should not be.

I have run out of curse words to describe my life right now, so I am making up new ones. The one for today: *swizzle-sticks*. I am in serious trouble.

~~~

The woman who screens guests at the prison is surprised to see me, "Hey, I wasn't expecting you back until Thursday."

"I know I'm sorry I didn't write in on the schedule. I need to finish my last session today because I will be out of town for the rest of this week. Is it okay if I meet with inmate number 589756 now?" I should get an Oscar for this performance.

She thinks for a moment, "Sure, I don't see why not.

I'll have a guard go and get him."

I make my way through security, get to cell 3B, and wait. I look a mess and I know it; I just hope it is not too obvious that I have been crying. After about ten minutes, a guard brings Jonah in and he looks surprised to see me.

He sits and says quietly, "What's wrong? You okay?"

Slowly I respond, "No Jonah." I look over to be sure the guard is out of earshot and continue, "I can't see you anymore, the last session is canceled."

This is harder than I thought.

His lashes flicker and his eyes open wide, "Why?" he drawls in a low voice, the word lingering in the air between us.

I do not answer, unsure of how to formulate the words. Before I can respond, Jonah quickly figures it out.

In a hushed whisper, he asks, "Did you lose your job?"

Fighting back the tears, I simply nod my head.

"Maddie I'm so sorry; was it because I didn't tell you sooner that I was not violent? Was it because I wrote you those notes?" He looks miserable as the words rush out.

"No, no it's nothing like that. You haven't done anything wrong. This was a mistake, though, allowing myself to cross boundaries with you. This was my fault. I need you to know that it is over. I won't be coming here to see you anymore, do you understand? I shouldn't have even come here to tell you this, I just wanted to see you one more time."

Jonah's lids lower and his shoulders fall as he lets a breath out, "Yes Maddie I understand. I'm sorry this happened but I would be lying if I said that I'm sorry I met you. These few moments with you have been the only good thing in my life for a long time and I will never regret it."

I say nothing, letting the unspoken words speak for themselves.

I look into his eyes, trying my best to take a mental picture of him; desperate to have his face in my memory forever.

"You're right though; you shouldn't have come here." Before I can comprehend the words, Jonah's lips are on mine. He is leaning over the table, careful not to let his chained wrists clank on the metal, the warmth of his mouth almost makes it all worth it, but I push him back.

"Jonah, please. Just go." Heartbroken and ashamed, I slump into the chair.

Wordlessly, Jonah leaves, and an emptiness hollows

out my body cavity, leaving me without air.

Chapter Eighteen

The guard coming in to check if I am done, is what finally compels me to get up to leave. Under a thick fog of self-pity and sadness, I pick up my briefcase, the weight of my choices settling down in my feet, making it difficult to move them. The world is closing in around me giving me tunnel vision, with the beating of my own heart being the only sound I hear.

I force myself to walk towards the opening of the cell.

Crumbling within myself, other sounds try to break through the thick barricade engulfing me, a foreign firecracker-like BANG slaps me back into awareness.

Stopping dead in my tracks, unfamiliar noises begin to fill my now razor-focused mind.

I hear indiscernible yelling and the sound of feet hitting concrete.

Something is not right.

I check for the guard, but he is nowhere.

A deafening CRACK of thunder suddenly fills the room around me, bouncing off the walls, reflecting off the metal surface of the table.

Gunfire.

This horrid realization pounds against the inside of my skull.

I peek out of the cell, spotting several inmates and guards, engaged in physical contact. Looks of panic spread across the guard's faces, one of them yelling in my direction "GET OUT OF HERE!"

An alarm begins to ring, WIRRRRRRRRRRR, followed by a booming voice repeating "CODE RED CODE RED."

Flashing red lights create an ominous atmosphere; reminding me of a haunted house I went through as a child.

A flurry of inmates run by, creating a blur of orange.

Fear envelops me and instinct kicks in as I contemplate my safety: should I hide, or should I try to run?

My gut tells me to run. As I get a few steps further out of the cell, I scan my surroundings and glance down into the commons area on the first floor where the majority of the disturbance appears to be taking place.

A watercolor of orange, gray, black, and red smear across the commons area. There is blood everywhere, on the walls, on the faces of guards and inmates, and streaked across the tables where the inmates normally eat.

The only people that are still amongst the commotion are the few that are laying on the floor and a couple sitting against the walls, hunched over.

Are they dead?

One guard is attempting to crawl as he cries out, "HELP, GET HELP!" but no one is listening.

Inmates have barricaded the main entryway and are chanting "KILL THE PIGS."

My heart beats harder and harder, pounding against my chest. Thud. Thud.

Unable to flee out the exit, I look in all directions, searching for somewhere to go.

A chill runs up my spine into the base of my neck . . .

I am being watched.

The sudden awareness of the possibility of rape inundates my mind. Maybe not just raped but killed. Panic vibrates through my body and my head throbs.

As long as I can escape with my life that is all that matters, I tell myself this as I flee back into cell 3B and try to hold the cell door closed.

Damn, I wish it had a lock from the inside.

Footsteps thump up the stairs and I know they are

coming for me.

I lean my entire body against the cell door, desperate to keep it closed, the heels of my feet sliding along the floor as it is pushed open.

"Haha, did you think that would work?" Asks the large white man with teardrop tattoos on his face looking at me as if I am food.

He exclaims to another, smaller Hispanic looking man, "A riot and pussy, today couldn't get any better."

The Hispanic man laughs a nasty laugh, "heeheheh."

They walk slowly towards me; I am breathing so hard and erratically that my lungs hurt. They enjoy my fear, taking their time, savoring the moment. For the first time in my life, I am prey.

I back up as far as I can go and grip the edge of the table. I must fight, so I rack my brain trying to remember the few moves I learned in a self-defense class when suddenly, a forceful, terrifying voice thrusts into the room.

"Get away from her!" Jonah screams through gritted teeth. He grips a large metal pipe. I knew Jonah was tall, but he appears taller now as he looks down at the men.

"The fuck man? We'll let you join in; you don't need

to have her all to yourself."

Jonah's jaw is tense as he shouts, "I said, get away from her, NOW!"

The men hesitate and the large white man gets irritated. He saunters toward Jonah with shoulders squared, "What the hell you gonna do about it, pretty boy?"

Jonah meets him face-to-face, not backing down, and says quietly, "Try me."

Taking him up on his offer, the man with the teardrop tattoos quickly pulls his right elbow back and brings his fist forward, just missing Jonah's face. The fight breaks out and Jonah swings back with the metal bar and slams it across his face, blood spurts across the room.

Two of the other men enjoy the confrontation so much, they are no longer interested in assaulting me, chanting "WOOT, WOOT, WOOT."

I take this opportunity to grab the keys from my briefcase, creating a makeshift weapon of my own.

Suddenly, a skinny man with no teeth pops into the cell yelling, "There's a door to the back open in block C and it is unguarded! We can escape mother fuckers, come on!"

The men do not hesitate and run out the door leaving the fight and me behind. Jonah rushes towards me; I curl on the ground with my knees to my chest, keys in my hand, wedged between my fingers.

His eyes soften, as he gets close, his voice is frantic as he says, "Come on Maddie," and just like that he lifts me over his shoulder and runs.

We run out the cell door, down to the commons area where the main entryway is still blocked.

Jonah yells above the fray, "There's a way out! Head out block C!"

Word about freedom spreads fast with men who spend their lives caged. The inmates start to fall away in a rush to get to the promised exit. A pack of ravenous wolves set free would be the only likeness I can compare the sight to. As soon as there are not enough inmates to keep the doors blocked, the guards bust them open and file in fully geared up with shields and guns. Behind the guards, an entire swat team pours in with jackets on them that have the word SWAT written in yellow on their backs.

Jonah throws the metal pipe aside and screams, "TAKE HER!"

Two members of the SWAT team grab me by my

elbows, pulling me off Jonah, swinging me back through the doors before I can process what is happening.

Looking back at Jonah, I see him tackled to the floor.

Chapter Nineteen

Standing outside of the prison walls, the sun beats down on the back of my neck. A police officer with kind eyes is talking to me as I try, in vain, to control my shaking body. A dull ache in my thigh leads me to reach down to touch it, causing the aching to get worse and develop into a pinching sensation.

Why is it wet?

Reaching for the curb of the parking lot to sit down, Officer Pete stops writing in his notepad to lend me a hand.

He takes this moment to ask me again to relax, "Miss, please, take it easy."

"Okay Officer, I just needed to sit down. I feel a bit dizzy."

I embrace the cold concrete and inch myself into a sitting position, determined to remain calm in front of Officer Pete.

"Ma'am, the ambulances are on the way, please stay seated until they get here and can assist you."

I reassure him, "Oh I am sure I don't need any help from the paramedics. I'm fine." Although I wish I would stop shaking.

Officer Pete leans down over me and gently puts his hand on my shoulder and in a quiet voice, says, "Ma'am, can you please lie down? You're injured and losing blood. I need you to lay down so that you do not hit your head if you lose consciousness."

"WHAT? I'm bleeding?"

I begin frantically looking all over my body and see that my right leg has a large pooling of blood staining my slacks. Now the pain begins to progress even further, moving from a pinching sensation to a sharp throbbing in a split second. The pain spreads all over my leg to where I am not able to distinguish the exact location of the injury.

"What happened?"

I look up into Officer Pete's kind eyes as he drops to one knee in front of me so that we are on the same level, "I'm still trying to figure that all out ma'am, but what I can say is that you have a bullet wound in your thigh. If you lay down, I'll apply pressure to stop the bleeding."

"Shot? I have been shot?"

Officer Pete's blurry face and jumbled words are the last things I remember.

Chapter Twenty

Light streams in my eyes forcing me to blink rapidly. I refocus my vision and see that I am in a hospital bed with wrappings covering my right leg and it is throbbing.

I am alone; left to sit with worry.

Is Jonah okay? Is my leg okay?

I reach down to touch my thigh, feeling around the bandages, noticing the spots of blood seeping through. My feet are bare; bloodstains inked down to my toes.

My body reacts and alarm sounds, beep, beep, beep, and nurses rush into the room. They try to comfort me. I am still groggy, unable to speak.

"The bullet entered through the back of your thigh,"

"It narrowly missed a major artery,"

"You've lost a lot of blood."

A person in a white coat tells me she spent four hours in emergency surgery to save my life and to stop the bleeding. I drift off, unable to fight the medication they have dosed me with.

~~~

Over the next few days in the hospital, I fade in and out of consciousness, waking only briefly to request more pain medication. By Sunday evening, the pain has begun to subside, and I am finally able to sit up in bed on my own, pulling out of the drug-induced grogginess. Medical professionals reassure me that the surgery went well, and I will be able to have complete use of my leg again.

The nurses remind me a few times of how lucky I am to have survived, "If the bullet was half an inch in another direction, the odds of surviving would have been minimal."

I am not sure why they think this will help me feel better, but I nod and smile knowing they are just trying to help. Six prison staff and eight inmates were not so lucky and lost their lives. Ten more suffered varying types of injuries, including bullet wounds, and stab wounds. The riot is the worst one in the prison's history and one of the worst for the entire state.

Henry, Tammy, Dr. Flanigan, and Min are by my hospital bedside Monday morning and I have never been happier to see them. Tammy brought flowers; further reminding me that I misjudged her. To my surprise, my father is not here but he does call to check on how I am doing every day.

Min has the most anxious look of them all and does

not want to leave my side, "I tried to see you a few times, but they wouldn't allow anyone who's not related to visit until you were more awake and had to ability to authorize visitors."

She is squeezing my hand so tight it hurts, but I do not tell her.

I am worried about Jonah and I can no longer refrain from asking, "Is Jonah okay?"

The question startles Henry as he says, "Jonah? Is that the inmate you have been working with?"

The looks on everyone's faces are priceless as I respond, "Yes, he saved my life."

Shocked, it takes a moment before anyone can respond.

"Oh, my Maddie, we didn't know," Dr. Flanigan expresses, eyes wide, "I'll check with the prison staff and find out his status." Dr. Flanigan grabs her phone and exits the room.

Looking confused Tammy asks, "What were you doing at the prison Maddie, and why didn't you tell us you had been fired? Can you tell us what happened?"

I know that there is no need to keep lying. I need to come clean. At this point, there is nothing more to lose.

"Did Dr. Flanigan tell you anything?" All the concerned faces staring back at me shake their heads.

"Well, that makes sense. For confidentiality purposes, it wouldn't be appropriate for her to tell all of you," I take a deep breath and continue, "I lost my job because I messed up. I continued the project without consulting with Dr. Flanigan about some information I found out about Jonah because I wanted to keep working with him."

The concerned faces change to confusion and before they can ask why, I jump in, "I made some poor ethical decisions and Dr. Flanigan found out and consulted with her boss who said I needed to be termed. Afterwards, I could not tell you all about what happened, I rushed out of the office before anyone could see me cry. I'm devastated by losing my job, but in light of everything that has happened, it seems small. To be honest, I was at the prison to see Jonah, I wanted to tell him in person that I had lost my job and that I could not finish the project."

Tammy scrunches her nose in confusion, "I don't understand Maddie, why would you need to tell him that? You could have just had the prison staff inform him that you wouldn't be coming back for the last session."

Clutching the thin blanket, the nurses gave me; I

breathe out and say, "I had to tell him in person Tammy. I had to because I'm in love with him."

The words are out of my mouth before I have time to think about what I am saying. It is the first time I am admitting this to myself. All four of their mouths drop.

"What," is said in unison.

"I know it is surprising and I know you all will not be able to understand but it's the truth and I don't want to try to deny it anymore. He saved my life; he is the bravest person I know, and I need to be brave too."

With eyes wide and mouth open, Henry quips, "Maddie he's a convict. He's never getting out of prison. What kind of relationship can you have with him?"

The ping of reality vibrates in my chest.

"I know Henry, I have thought about all of that as well. That is why I have been so ashamed of how I feel; I have even been seeing a therapist about it. However, even if I never get to see him outside of prison walls, I still love him. We may not be able to be in a real relationship and we both know that; it does not change the way I feel about him."

A weight on my chest lifts slightly with this revelation.

"Maddie this makes all of the research you did invalid, you know that right?" asks Henry. "It could jeopardize all of the work we have done." His words dripping with pity and annoyance.

"Yes, I know Henry. I'm so sorry about this. I'm not the type of person to do anything unethical but I am not sure who I am anymore. I just hope that the rest of the research you all did will be enough to finish the project and that the F.B.I. will be satisfied with the work. I know that all of the work I did will need to be scrapped."

Henry, clearly feeling bad for me, and says, "Maddie, I care about you, I'm sorry you were hurt but I don't know what to say. You may have cost us everything, all our research, this entire project—may need to be thrown out. I just can't believe this. I thought you had more sense. I had no idea you were so selfish. I'm sorry, I have to go. Good luck with everything Maddie, I hope you learn from this."

Henry walks out of the room, taking any self-respect I had left with him.

Tammy and Min just look at me, pity etched into their faces.

Dr. Flanigan walks back into the room and smiles, "He

is just fine Maddie, in fact, the warden wants to speak with you about what happened. They have it all on security cameras and need a witness statement from you. I'm sure it is also to assess whether you will be filing a lawsuit against the prison. The warden will be stopping by the hospital later today along with some of his staff."

I do not hear much after she utters the words "he is just fine," and am so relieved that my breathing noticeably improves. The fear that he had been injured or killed was disturbing every molecule in my body.

"Thank you, Dr. Flanigan."

"Where did Henry go?"

"He left. He's upset with me because I told him why I got fired and I also told him that I am in love with Jonah."

Dr. Flanigan's eyes go wide, "You're in love with him?"

"Yes. I'm just trying to be honest since I have been lying so much lately. I don't want to do that anymore."

"Maddie, I'm worried about you, I don't know what you have been thinking lately but I am glad you weren't killed. I better go as well; I have work to do."

Dr. Flanigan walks out, leaving just Tammy and Min.

~~~

"I will go grab you a coffee from the café I saw on the first level. I'll be right back," says Min, leaving Tammy to say her piece.

The increased wrinkling between Tammy's brows tells me she is serious, "Maddie, I am so glad you are okay, but what you did was risky. You should not have gone to the prison without approval. What you did was very unprofessional."

"I know Tammy. I've been acting crazy lately."

Tammy looks down in contemplation, and I realize the one person I used to think was the biggest loser, is the only person offering me the empathy that I do not deserve. "At the beginning of this project Dr. Flanigan told us all, that developing a personal relationship with an inmate was the worst thing we could do. I'm disappointed and surprised by this Maddie. It's so unlike you. Now that I've said what needed to be said; I wanted to tell you that I'm so glad that you're okay. When I got the call, my heart sank. Please let me know if there is anything I can do for you. I know we have not been great friends or anything, but I hope you know that I am here for you if you need anyone to talk to."

I sigh, "Thanks, Tammy. Thanks for your kindness, I don't deserve it. I'm sorry I haven't always been kind to you, and I've laughed when Dave or Henry have teased you. I never gave you a chance. The thing is, you're right, this whole thing is so unlike me. I can't explain it to you because I do not even understand it myself yet. I don't know what is going on with me but, right now I am just glad to be alive. I want to take this opportunity to rethink my life. This project has taught me a lot, including the fact that I still have a lot to learn about human behavior. Hell, maybe I will take this opportunity to go back to school to get my Ph.D. I want to learn more, much more. I feel like I have been given a second chance at life."

Tammy smiles, "That's a great idea, Maddie. If you need a professional reference, please don't hesitate to ask me."

Surprised by her offer I smile back and say, "Thank you so much."

She hugs me before she heads out the door; I revel over how I never saw her for who she really was.

~~~

After Min and Tammy leave, I get a frantic phone call from my father. He is glad to hear that I am awake and says he has been calling the hospital daily, waiting for me to be well enough to talk to him on the phone.

"Why didn't you just drive here dad?"

He only lives an hour away but is in poor health. Even still, it surprises me that he is not by my side.

"Well, I wanted to dear, but it is not easy for me to drive anymore. I should have taken the bus though. Can you forgive me for not coming?"

"Yes of course dad, I'm just happy to be alive and to be speaking with you now. I'll keep you posted on my recovery."

After we hang up, I get a sense that something was off with him but decide to ignore it.

Just as Dr. Flanigan warned, at around three p.m. there's a knock at my hospital room door, and in walks the Warden from North Branch.

"Hello Ms. Tilltot, can we speak with you for a moment?"

He is already in the room, not giving me a choice, "Sure, I guess so."

The warden walks to the chair beside my bed followed by two other men, who linger towards the back of the room.

The warden's steps are heavy, as though his body is carrying the weight of the inmates at his prison on his back. His baldhead is speckled with a few wisps of white hairs, his face marred by deep creasing along his brow bone, leaving his face with a permanent scowl. He greets me with a firm handshake.

While chewing slowly on a toothpick he says, "First Ms. Tilltot, I wanted to know how you were feeling."

"I'm well, I was told I am going to be fine, but I have to stay in the hospital a few more days before I can head home."

"I see, well I'm glad to hear that. I'm here because we need to get a full statement from you about what happened. Can you do that for me?"

"Yes."

"Ok great, this'll be recorded."

I sit up in my bed and prepare myself to tell the story. I start with who I am and discuss the research project that we were working on and I explain that the reason I am at the prison, was to work on the project.

"I was not originally scheduled to be there that day, but I was not going to be available for the scheduled time that week, so I went early." I think it best to lie about why I was there; it does not seem like it is something these people should know.

"As soon as the meeting finished, inmate Jonah left with a guard, and about two minutes later a commotion started. I went to leave but was unable to get out because inmates were blocking the way out, several inmates barricaded me into cell 3B, intending to assault me. Inmate Jonah came into the room and stopped them by threatening them. He had a weapon, a metal bar, and was involved in a brief altercation with one of the inmates before the men then fled, as another inmate told them that there was a way out. Inmate Jonah then threw me over his shoulder and ran over to the doors where the inmates were blocking the entry. As soon as we got there, a swat team was able to barge in and inmate Jonah handed me over to the swat team so that I could get to safety. It was during this transaction that I was probably struck by the stray bullet."

I ended the retelling by stating, "Inmate Jonah M. truly saved my life."

The three men were entranced as I told the story, in disbelief, one is taking notes while I speak and since he is in a suit, I presume he is the lawyer.

The warden responds, "That's what we thought had happened Ms. Tilltot. We have been studying the security footage and witnessed most of the scene except for what happened inside the cell, as the cell was out of the camera's visual. We saw you try to leave; we saw the men rush you back into the cell and then we saw the inmate Jonah enter. We can see the inmates and Jonah leave after a few moments with you on his shoulder. We were shocked by what appeared to be going on as it looked as though Jonah took you out of the cell and over to the SWAT team to get you to safety. Just so you know, not only did inmate number 589756, Jonah M., save your life but he also saved potentially many more. As he was walking with the guard back to his cell after the meeting with you was finished, he witnessed inmate number 67854 give a signal to a group of inmates in the commons area. Jonah was aware of what the signal meant, so, he turned to Eric, the guard walking him back to his cell, and warned him that a riot was about to start. Eric was able to send an emergency signal to the control tower. That gave advanced notice that a riot was about to break out, which enabled us to take preventative measures, including quickly notifying SWAT."

Wow.

He continues, "If we didn't have that information, the response would not have been as immediate. Inmate Jonah M. played a major part in preventing what could have been an even worse tragedy. We have him in seclusion now because the other inmates know what he did, and they will kill him if they get the opportunity. They're calling him a traitor and nark, now his life could be in grave danger."

The heaviness in my chest returns as I hear this.

"You have to understand how incredibly unusual this is Ms. Tilltot. I've since learned his case is up for retrial and I plan to bring up these actions at his trial myself by offering this information during character witness testimony. I hope that what he did Friday will help him to lower his sentence and maybe get out of prison sooner than he expected."

I was not expecting to hear this. Perhaps I could provide character witness testimony as well. I make a mental note to look into it after I leave the hospital.

"That's great to hear Warden. Would it be possible for me to see him? I'd like to thank him in person."

Please let me see him, I beg internally.

"Yes Ms. Tilltot, that can be arranged, no problem," the warden casually responds.

The next part of the conversation involves the warden stating the prison will pay my medical expenses if I agree not to file a lawsuit. I explain that would be fine, as long as my medical expenses are covered then I am happy.

When the men leave my hospital room, I sit in disbelief. Not only did Jonah risk his own life to save mine, but he also warned the guards about the impending riot. A sliver of hope starts to creep up my spine as I allow myself to think that maybe, just maybe, Jonah will get out of prison and we could have a future together.

~~~

As I sit alone in my hospital bed, overcome again by emotions, I burst into tears. I cry for the fear I felt in those moments, I cry out of relief to be alive, I cry for Jonah, I cry for myself. I wonder about what lead Jonah back to check on me; did he worry that I had not left the facility yet? Did he see the men push their way into the cell with me? Was he waiting to watch me leave? Or did he run back to the cell just in case I was still there?

A sense of newness washes over me as I contemplate how I will now rebuild my life. The cloud that I have been under since my divorce lifts, allowing light to peek into the dark that has shrouded me these last few months.

Chapter Twenty-One

The time spent in the hospital is a blur. Nurses and the physician come in and out constantly and within a few short days, I am up on my feet walking, but I will not be able to drive for another week.

During my stay in the hospital, Min is a regular, stopping by every evening after she gets off work. She brings me fast food, so I do not have to eat the dreadful hospital food and keeps me company. She understands as I talk about Jonah. She thinks it is only natural that I have fallen in love with him after he saved my life. She does not fully understand that I had already fallen in love with him before the riot. It is too hard for her to believe.

On the day of my release, Min drives me home and asks me about Jonah. We have been talking about how I should thank him, but I am yet undecided.

"So, you decide how to thank Jonah yet?"

I shrug, "No, I haven't. Did I tell you that the warden called me this morning and I have a meeting set up with him tomorrow at noon? I still do not know what I'm going to say when I see him. They have him in a secluded part of the prison as protection from the other inmates.

They may have to relocate him to another prison. Far enough away, that nobody will have heard about what he did. I hope that it'll help him get through this if he sees me in person."

Min shakes her head in disbelief, "Wouldn't being secluded be hard? Is he alone all the time?"

I nod, "Yes, I think it's hard. I'm really worried about him."

She nods with understanding and goes on, "You know Maddie, maybe by just seeing him and saying thank you is enough."

"I know you don't want me to get involved with him Min, thank you for still being my friend even though you disagree with what I am doing."

"Of course. I'm no fair-weather friend. How are you getting to the prison tomorrow?"

"Tammy is nice enough to take me. I appreciate the help you all have been giving me. I can't wait to get back to driving."

Min laughs, "Always so anxious Maddie. It's just for another week. Just focus on relaxing and healing. The driving will come soon enough."

~~~

The next day, Tammy picks me up at eleven and drives me to the prison. It works out well because she needs to meet with the inmate she has been working with to follow up on a few things, so she arranges to do so while I meet with Jonah.

This time when I enter the prison, they escort me to a different area because my near assault is a hot topic and the guards do not want me to be seen.

I wait in a room that has two chairs bolted to the ground. Unlike the room I used before, this one has no table and no window. The gray walls give me chills. At least the cell I used to conduct interviews in had a small window, now I understand that even though that window had bars on it, it is still better than no window at all.

I sit and wait for Jonah, nervous, but not as much as I normally am before I see him. Instead, I am excited, goosebumps cover my arms and the back of my neck. I want to tell him I love him, but I know that is not a good idea. I am also not under the illusion that Jonah feels the same way about me. With him locked up, I do not know if he would even want to know how I feel about him since there is not anything that he can offer me.

As these thoughts filter through my head, Jonah walks

in causing them all to fade away in an instant. He lets out a sigh when he sees me as if he has been holding his breath. His eyes light up and he quickly scans down to my leg. His face changes from joy to concern as he takes a seat next to me. He can move his hands and legs around freely; the shackles are gone. A guard walks with him but does not hold on to his arm like they used to.

The guard walks out and before he shuts the door behind him, he turns and asks me if I am okay being with Jonah alone and I respond, "Absolutely."

"Okay," he says, "if you need anything there is a button on the arm of your chair that will alert me to come in. You have just five minutes before I have to take him back." With that, he pulls the door shut behind him.

Jonah looks at my leg and rubs his chin slowly, "The inmates may want to kill me, but the guards treat me way better. I think they trust me now. It's crazy."

He leans back in the chair and smiles. I take a deep breath before I begin to speak, trying to calm my heartbeat, worried he can hear it.

"Jonah, I wanted to come here and see you in person as soon as I was able to get out of the hospital. I want to say thank you. Thank you for saving my life. I wish I could express to you how grateful I am for your actions that day."

My voice quivers as I say this so I stop speaking otherwise I know I will cry.

He looks at me with soft eyes and says, "Of course I would save you, Maddie. You don't have to thank me. How are you, by the way, the warden told me you had been shot in the thigh but wouldn't tell me much about it."

I glance down at my fingers laced together, "I'm doing just fine. I can't drive for a little while but overall, I'm great. I have quite a few stitches and had to have surgery, but I'm lucky. Or at least that is what they keep telling me."

He watches me speak as though he is unsure about how to respond.

I pause and he says, "I was so worried Maddie; they wouldn't tell me anything for days. I have never been so scared in my entire life."

My heart swells.

"Me neither Jonah. Please tell me though, how did it happen? Why did you come back to the cell?"

Jonah runs his hand through his hair and explains,

"When Eric was taking me back to my cell, I saw the signal given by one of the gangs indicating that a riot was about to start. I heard talks of it for some time and knew the plan, but I didn't know when it was going down. Once I realized there was a possibility you were still in the building, I told Eric. He had just taken off my handcuffs but hadn't locked my cell door yet. I would've gotten to you sooner, but Eric was trying to hold me back, but wasn't able to for long because some inmates were coming at him trying to take his weapons. I kinda hated to leave him in that situation but I was more worried about you. I grabbed a pipe that was laying on the floor and when I saw the men go in the cell, I knew you must be in there. I'm so sorry that happened. I hope they didn't touch you."

"You don't need to apologize, Jonah, you saved me and just in time. No, those men didn't have a chance to touch me. They had been laughing and were talking about raping me when you burst in."

Jonah shakes his head and looks agitated. "I know what they were trying to do Maddie. I hate those guys."

His sudden change to anger startles me a little and when he sees this, he softens again, "Sorry, Maddie. I don't mean to scare you. It just really angered me."

"It's okay Jonah. Was Eric hurt?"

Jonah runs his hand through his hair and says, "He'll live."

I am very aware of the fact that we are alone when I notice Jonah glimpse towards the door before turning back at me, "I may never have a chance like this again and I don't want to miss it."

I look at him quizzically, his hand running through his hair again and he bites his lower lip, "Can I kiss you again Maddie?"

My mouth drops open and I inhale sharply. All I manage to do is nod.

He leans forward in his chair until we are close enough that I can feel his breath; erratic but warm. As he presses his lips to mine, electricity sparks down to the tips of my toes. After a beat, he opens his mouth for a deeper kiss, tasting me as I taste him, minty with a hint of sweetness. His hand is on my face and his thumb is gently caressing my cheek. His tongue grazes mine and I think that at this moment, I might be the happiest I have ever been.

He stops, leans back slightly, and with wide eyes, he

whispers fervently, "Damn Maddie, you are killing me."

The cell door creeks and we quickly retreat.

The guard walks in casually, "Ready?"

Jonah stands to leave but before he leaves the room, he turns to me and says, "I know you came here to thank me Maddie, but it should be me thanking you. You have brought me back to life and have given me hope. So, for that, I thank you."

I am too out of sorts to respond and he walks out, taking the air in the room with him.

I have tasted happiness; rode high on the wave of pure joy, and now my heart aches as I wonder if I will ever be that high again.

~~~

At home, I write a letter.

Jonah- seeing you today was incredible. Before the riot, I had every intention of removing you from my life completely. I was angry with myself for allowing you to have an impact on me, angry for allowing myself to be so caught up that I lost my job. Then you saved me, and all of that anger is gone. You have opened my eyes. I see you for who you really are. You are not some common criminal. You are so much more than that and I am sorry I was ever ashamed to admit that I am attracted to you. I have learned some hard lessons and am still learning. I want to show you how grateful I am for you. I want you to understand. I do not know how to convey my gratitude. There are not enough words in the English language. You asked me if we could write to each other and I said no. I have changed my mind and want you as a friend and a pen pal for as long as you will let me. – Maddie

Chapter Twenty-Two

Over the next few days, I do not leave my house. Instead, I sit and think. Now that I do not have a job, this is a perfect time to create a new life plan. I throw myself into looking at graduate schools so that I can pursue a Ph.D. in Forensic Psychology. A few make my list including William James College in Massachusetts and Walden University that offer online courses. Luckily, I have plenty of money saved up from working at the F.B.I. and the sum I received my divorce settlement so that I can go six months living on what I have without any income.

Come Thursday, I am ecstatic to see that I have a letter from Jonah.

Maddie - Thank you for your letter. I am thrilled that you want to write to me. I was hoping for this. I have some news. I am being moved to North Dakota State Penitentiary in Bismarck. The move is happening on Monday. The Warden and my lawyer are worried about my mental state if I remain secluded for much longer and they cannot release me back into the general population because my life is in danger here. It is harder than I ever imagined. I am alone for 23 hours a day. It is torture. I am excited to be around people again even if they are convicts. This means I will not see you until my trial. Would you come? I would love to have you there. It is April so that leaves around 22 weeks until then. That is a long time to go without seeing you. I had started to get used to seeing your face. I hope that you can send me your picture in your next letter? Not a dirty one or anything (unless you want . . .). I am trying not to get my hopes up about my trial. I know that it is not likely that I will get a lower sentence, but I can't help but think what if? If I were getting out, would you see me? Could we have a relationship? You don't have to answer that if it is too hard. Let me know how your job hunt goes and what your plan is. I hope your leg is healing well. Also, when you write me back, use the address and inmate number I wrote on the back of this letter for the new prison. P.S. I would give anything to kiss you again.- Jonah

Pained that I will not be able to see his face again for so long, I set the letter down and sigh.

Chapter Twenty-Three

I spend the afternoon trying to take the perfect selfie to put in with the letter I wrote to Jonah. I put on my best outfit and fix my hair. I probably take at least fifty pictures and hate all of them. I finally land on one and use my portable printer, link it to my phone and print off the small portrait.

Jonah - I hope you like the picture although I am sorry to report that it is not dirty. I am happy to share that my leg is healing, and I am to be cleared to drive by my doctor early next week. How was your transfer? That had to be a long trip. Do you have a cellmate? What is he like? Are you safe? I hate that I will have to wait so long to see you as well. I only have your mug shot to look at and you look sad in it. And yes, I will be at your trial, I have to see you.

By the way, I noticed today when I was going through your file again that your birthday was April 26th. Why didn't you tell me?! Happy belated 27th birthday. Twenty-seven is so young. I forget how young you are because you seem so much older. To help get through the weeks, keep writing. You are a very talented writer. If you finish any new stories, send them to me. I would be honored to read them. As for your questions about if we could have a relationship if you were out of prison, I think it best I do not answer that. I want to enjoy the relationship we do have, not dwell on what we don't. Also, I am trying not to get my hopes up about your trial as well . . . P.S. I dream about that kiss every night. – Maddie

~~~

The days wear on with little occurrence; I get visits from Min, think about Jonah and spend a lot of time thinking about my mom, which surprises me. My recent brush with death initially sparked a sensation of being ready for anything, being happy to be alive but it does not take long for those feelings fade. Even with my newfound excitement, I am still missing something, but I am not sure what it is.

I start seeing Dr. Abby again so she can help me process my jumbled bag of emotions. I talk a lot about my mother but am too nervous to bring up my love for Jonah. I am worried that Dr. Abby will tell me I'm wrong, and I don't want to be.

"Maddie, you've been through so much in such a short amount of time. You're in shock, traumatized, scared. Of course, you're thinking about your mother, you need her now more than ever. I'm not too sure you ever really dealt with losing her, to begin with. You've never really let her go. It might be a good time for you to head home to visit your father and childhood home. This may help you feel close to your mother again. Plus, it'll also help if you had some family support after so much trauma."

"Head home? You don't understand Dr. Abby, my father and I are not exactly close. Ever since my mother died, I feel like we just don't know how to talk to each other. I think visiting him would just be awkward for us both."

"Maddie, what better time in your life than now to work on that relationship?" Ugh, she is so annoying sometimes. Especially when she is right.

"Okay, I'll think about it."

"We're at the end of the session and I wanted to bring something up with you before you leave Maddie."

"What's that?"

"You said to me before that you couldn't be really interested in someone like Jonah, a criminal. You seemed to have a substantial feeling of shame around this crush of yours. Do you still feel that way now that he saved your life?"

"No Dr. I'm not ashamed of it now."

"Maddie, what are your feelings towards him now?"

"Look Dr., I know what you're going to say. I know this doesn't make sense."

"Maddie, please be honest with me and tell me what you're feeling, or I can't help you."

I sigh, "Well...to be honest...I think I'm in love with him. He's so much more than what I thought, I mean he's brave and cares for me, he risked everything to help me."

"I see. Maddie, I need to be honest with you so please listen to what I have to say with an open mind."

Here it comes.

"Your feelings of what you believe to be love may not be love. It's natural for you to have such a strong reaction towards him, especially after he saved your life. But I don't want you to confuse that with real love. This person is not realistic for you Maddie. You need to remember that. This man is not right for you. This is not the love that you need in your life."

I leave Dr. Abby's office deflated, is she right? How

could something so powerful not be right?

Chapter Twenty-Four

It is a Thursday afternoon as I sit in my apartment with a book. The spring sun is filtering in through my window, beckoning me to do something other than keep myself locked inside this room. Even the twenty-somethings' that live next door are in the front of the building enjoying the weather while listening to some music and drinking mid-day margaritas.

Do they not have jobs?

I think about how it has been quite some time since I have heard from Jonah. Flipping my book shut, I put my shoes on and head over to Dr. Abby's office for my appointment. I bring up my anxiety about Jonah with Dr. Abby, and she patiently sits and listens.

"He said he wanted to write letters to each other, so I wrote him one and he responded. However, I wrote to him again and I haven't heard back. He's probably unable to write because he was in the process of being transported to another prison so he would be safer, but I'm just surprised it has taken him this long to write back, I guess. What do you make of that Dr. Abby?"

She responds carefully, "Madeline, I don't want to beat

around the bush, so I will get straight to it. You not hearing from Jonah for weeks at a time is somewhat of a reality check for you as this would be typical if you were to continue this correspondence with him. He cannot offer you anything more. That is something you need to think about, as I said last time, this is not right for you."

"I know Dr. Abby. I know you think that but it's hard for me to see. I am just so overwhelmed by my feelings towards him. I mean, I know he's a prisoner and can't be with me in real life, but I still thought he would write more."

"Maddie, do you want a relationship with someone that would involve you sitting around waiting for letters from him? Or do you want a real relationship?"

"I wish you would beat around the bush more Dr. Abby. I don't think I care for this direct, honest approach."

Dr. Abby laughs, "Maddie, have you given anymore thought to going back home to visit with your dad? I really think it would be good for you. You need support Maddie, now especially."

Ugh, maybe she's right.

~~~

I check my mail as soon as I get home and see a letter from North Dakota. I feel ridiculous at how excited I am to tear it open and read it even before I make it into the apartment.

Maddie – I am sorry it has been a while since I have written to you. The transfer was long, but I am glad to be here but it has been a hard adjustment. I have a cellmate, Frankie. He is chill and we get along. I do believe I am safe, or at least as safe as I can be in a prison. I will keep writing stories while I am in here; I have to keep sane. If I write anything that is not too embarrassing, I will send it your way. I didn't tell you about my birthday because I don't care about birthdays. I have never had anyone celebrate my birthday before, so I don't even think about it. It was just another day for me. One-time Zeek took me out to the beach on my birthday. That was the best birthday I ever had. We laid in the sand drinking a bottle of vodka he'd stole from the liquor store. It was disgusting but we didn't care. I am not surprised you think I seem older than twenty-seven because I feel so much older. By the way, is it rude to ask? How old are you? I assume you are not married because you have never mentioned it and you do not wear a ring, but have you been married? You have never mentioned kids. If you don't have any, do you want any? If I ever get out of here, I want a family. I have never had one and I want one. It doesn't have to be a big one or anything, just a wife and at least one kid. And a job. And a dog. Maybe a cat but I would prefer a dog. If I do get out, I don't know what I would do for money. I guess some programs can help me and I hope that is true. What about you? Where do you see yourself being 5 or 10 years from now? What do you want out of life? Look forward to hearing from you soon and that picture you sent me is beautiful. Frankie is jealous. – Jonah

Lying in bed, I stare at the ceiling and ponder about how funny life is. Here I was, for so many years so sure of myself. I viewed life as simple, I followed a life plan and I made good choices that led to a successful career. Now I lay here, single, unemployed, and completely lost. What is the point of all this anyway? It is our accomplishments that matter most, or is it the connections that we make? I used to believe that the key to happiness was accomplishing life goals. Perhaps happiness is not as simplistic as I previously believed. Perhaps happiness ebbs and flows and builds upon itself. Perhaps it is all about a feeling. What is it that makes me feel good? The birds chirping outside my window in the morning makes me feel good. The warmth of a freshly brewed cup of coffee makes me feel good. A simple letter from someone who just wants to know me makes me feel good.

Unable to sleep, I sit up and reread Jonah's story about the invisible boy. Wanting to reach out to him, I write a letter.

Jonah- it is not rude for you to ask. I am thirty-three years old and divorced and no, I don't have children. I always figured I would have two children, a boy, and a girl. Now that I am divorced and unemployed, I am not so sure about anything anymore. I live in a small apartment alone and could probably benefit from a pet. Maybe I will get a dog. It sounded nice when you mentioned it. I think I might be having a life crisis. My entire world has come crashing down around me and it is forcing me to look at what I want out of life. I don't know where I see myself in five years. If you had asked me that five years ago, I would have told you my entire life plan. Now, I am not so sure. What did you want to be when you were a kid? I know you did not end up where you planned, or did you have a plan? Since all this change has happened and I am no longer working, I keep thinking that I should use this as an opportunity for reflection but that does not provide any immediate answers.

I wish you were here with me now, laying by my side in my bed as I write this. I do miss you, Jonah. I miss hearing your voice and seeing the flecks of gold in your green eyes but mostly, I miss the way you make me feel. I hope that can bring you some sense of peace while you are locked away. – Maddie

Chapter Twenty-Five

That next morning, I drop my letter to Jonah into the mail bin, and my phone buzzes. It is my father calling again and I contemplate ignoring it. He keeps calling me, but I am never sure what to say to him.

The phone buzzes again and I open the car door and sit inside. Dr. Abby's recommendation to head home rings in my head. It might be good for me to go home; it has been a long time. I let the call go to voicemail and drive back to my apartment so I can pack an overnight bag.

My father has lived in the same house he bought with my mother during their first year of marriage and will leave it to me when he passes, at one point asking me to consider living there after he dies to which I told him I would never. While I love the home, my work is based around the F.B.I. headquarters so I always figured I would sell it. Now that I am no longer with the F.B.I. I do not know what I will do with the house, but I doubt I will keep it and live there, as it was never part of my plan to end up living in my hometown. As I think this, it dawns on me that maybe I need to throw out the rest of my life plan since it is blown to bits anyway.

Living without a plan? How would that even work?

With my father's health in decline, I have been apprehensive to see him. I always have an underlying sense of fear about what I will do once I lose him because he is the only family I have left. My grandparents died when I was very young, and both of my parents were only children, so I never had any uncles, aunts, or cousins. I have some distant relatives, but my parents were never close with them, so I have never known any of them. The idea of having no family leaves me crestfallen so I force the thought out of my head, convincing myself that my father is not going to die anytime soon. To complicate this trip home, I have not yet told him that I have lost my job with the F.B.I.; he is a retired professor whom I admire vehemently. The last thing I want is for him to be disappointed in me.

Fredrick, Maryland is a town of about seventy thousand people and is your typical east coast town. Nothing special, nothing out of the ordinary. It is an old town with civil war era buildings but still manages to have a modern feel.

Truthfully, I love Frederick. It will always be my favorite town. I was happy growing up there and I have wonderful memories of my mother. While it is painful to go back and think so much of her, it also brings me a sense of tranquility. It almost seems like she is still alive when I am home. Her presence is all around me.

I pull up to my family home and park in the paved driveway. The neighborhood looks the same with its charming homes and tall chestnut oak trees lining the street. The streetlights are elaborate and resilient with a look as though they are from another time, a time of elegance. It is not quite noon and I walk up the porch steps and look over to the white swing I used to practically live on as a child.

The warm air settles on my shoulders, reminding me of summer evenings; swinging back and forth on the porch swing; watching for fireflies; dreaming of my future.

Dad must sense me because he opens the door and says, "Maddie!" even before I knock. We embrace and he still smells the same. Like cigars and cardigans.

"Hey Dad, how are you?"

"How am I? You're the one who was shot Maddie, how the hell are you?" He says incredulously.

"I'm okay, I'm getting around fine," I say trying to

sound nonchalant.

"I'm so relieved to hear that Maddie, that was the scariest phone call I've ever received. Please come in and I'll make lunch."

We walk in and the screen door slams behind us; the cracking of the frame so familiar to me that I momentarily feel ten years old again; a simple sound transporting me to another time.

Not much has changed except the house is surprisingly messy. The same dusty books stacked in piles up against the banister of the staircase, something that mother would never have tolerated, and the antique bronze lamp with a teal blue Tiffany shade is still on the small side table in the corner of the entryway. What is unusual is the random clothes lying across the staircase steps.

"Dad, you doing okay? The house is a bit of a mess."

"Oh yes, I was just not expecting you back. You should have called and told me you were coming so I could've picked up a bit."

Something is not right about his response; my father has always kept the house the same after mom passed except for his collection of books lying around.

"How long are you back for Maddie?"

"Only a couple of day's dad."

"Oh. Well at least I get to see you even if it is brief."
The familiar sting of guilt rears its head again.

"I'd love to stay longer dad, but I can't," he waves me
off as if to tell me not to worry about it.

"What would you like for lunch? I can make a
sandwich with some pasta salad."

"Sounds great, let me help though."

I turn the corner to the kitchen; shock slaps me across
the face.

Empty delivery boxes and piled up dishes reveal a
house that is more than just messy. The smell of garbage
and rotting food engulf my nostrils as I notice the full
trash bags leaning against a full trash can; a bug scurrying
across the counter catches my eye.

Dad walks to the fridge to pull out sandwich items, I
notice green residue on the bread, and my heart drops to
the pit of my stomach.

Several pill bottles are pushed back along the, what
used to be, white backsplash and I can tell immediately
that they are all full of pills.

The bottles and the backsplash are so dusty they look
gray and my concern grows, "Dad, are you taking your

meds?"

My father was diagnosed with Huntington's disease when he was in his forties. The disease is brutal causing nerve cells break down over time. There is no cure, but you can treat it with drugs and physical therapy. It has been devastating for my father especially after mom died. The disease will cause cognitive and physical problems including mental confusion, problems with coordination, and loss of muscle among other horrible symptoms.

"Uh, listen Maddie. I don't think those pills are helping me anymore, so I stopped taking them."

Stunned I continue, "What do you mean dad? The doctor said you have to take them."

"Eh, don't worry about it, dear. Now let me make you some lunch."

After a moment of contemplation, I say, "It's okay. I just ate before I got here."

"Oh okay. Well, in that case, I'm going to go lay down for a bit Maddie, please make yourself comfortable."

Dread washes over me. I cannot leave him here like this. I will have to stay until I can get something figured out. Maybe a caregiver or a nurse or something.

As I mull over my father's health and what I can do to

help, I go through and begin cleaning the house; the only thing I can think to do. I cannot let my father live like this.

In the corner on the countertop, I see what looks to be mouse droppings and more insects; I run my index finger over the granite slab, a trail follows my finger, showing my path clearly.

With a deep breath, I take a quick walk around the rest of the house and everything has a layer of dust except for his recliner in the living room, "This is going to take me all day, hell maybe all week," I say aloud to myself.

This cannot be happening. I am not ready to lose him. I am so wrapped up in myself that I missed the signs that he needed help.

I scold myself, "I should've come back sooner."

Chapter Twenty-Six

Over the next couple of days, I begin to see the full extent of my father's condition.

When I get a chance to talk with Connie, the next-door neighbor who has been friends with my father since she moved in, she explains, "Dear, I am so glad you are back. I asked your father for your phone number because I wanted to call you and let you know that he is not doing well but he refused to give it to me. Honestly, I do not believe he has left that house in months. I only see him sitting on the porch swing occasionally, and that is it. I have not seen his car leave once. I have been going and getting him groceries about once a week, but that is all the help he will accept from me. Sometimes when I try to speak with him, he seems nervous and confused."

"Okay, thank you for telling me. I had no idea that he was doing this poorly. I should've come back sooner to check on him. He just never let on when I talk with him on the phone. I don't know what I'm going to do. I'm looking into seeing if I can get him a nurse or caregiver to help him."

"Oh yes, I understand Maddie. I just worry that your

father is so stubborn that he will just send the nurse away once you leave. You know how he is dear."

"Yes, I know Connie. I'm worried about the same thing."

It has become apparent that it is not safe to leave my father here at the house alone, he wanders around confused and has forgotten to shut doors and turn off the stove several times since I have arrived.

During the week, I get everything organized. I clean the house top to bottom, I get dad scheduled for regular physical therapy sessions, and I can get him back on his meds after some major convincing and begging on my part.

At the first doctor's appointment he has had in six months, the doctor tells me that dad is deteriorating at a rapid rate and he requires full-time care and recommends a nursing home.

With my own life recently falling apart, maybe I should stay in Frederick to take care of him. I do not want him to go to a nursing home, not yet, because, at sixty, he is still too young.

When we get back home after the appointment, dad is silent as he goes inside. I stay outside and sit on the porch swing, considering moving in full time with dad, when I get a call from Min.

"Hey, where have you been? I haven't heard from you in a while."

"Min, I'm in Frederick, with my dad. He's not doing well, and the doctor told me he needs 24/7 care."

"Oh, Maddie are you serious? I'm so sorry to hear that. What're you going to do?"

"Well, I'm considering moving in with him and be his caretaker."

"Wow, that's a big job. Are you up for something like that?"

"I don't know, but I think it's the right thing to do. I mean, I don't have a job with the F.B.I. anymore. It is not like I have much of a life I would be leaving behind. Maybe all of this was meant to happen or something."

"Well, I think that if that is what you need to do then you should. What can I do to help? Do you need me to bring you your stuff?"

Grateful she offered so I would not have to ask, I say, "Actually if it is not too much to ask, I could use some more clothes. I only brought enough for two days."

"No problem Maddie, I can come tomorrow. I will call

you when I am at your place to see what you want me to pack."

"Perfect, do you still have the spare key?"

"Sure do."

"Thanks, Min you're the best."

"I know, I'll see you tomorrow."

~~~

The next day, Min calls as she is packing up clothes and some of my personal items and, to say thanks, I tell her I will cook her dinner. She loves my lasagna and garlic bread, which happens to be the only dish that I can make well. Dad is excited to see Min; he has always liked her, but then again everybody likes Min. He is having a good day, so I anticipate this to be a good evening.

When she arrives, Min hugs my dad and he asks, "Hi Min, how's Raymond and Lizzy?"

I am delighted that he remembers Min's family, as his failing cognitive abilities have been apparent over the last week, with him often forgetting what he ate for breakfast or even once forgetting where his bedroom was.

The three of us spend the next few hours chatting about Min's work and daughter, and around five p.m. dad goes upstairs to take a quick nap and Min takes the opportunity to say discreetly, "Maddie, you were right. Your dad is struggling. I've never seen him like this. I hate it."

"I know I'm devastated. I had no idea it had gotten this bad. I should've visited him more. I feel terrible about it."

"Don't be so hard on yourself Maddie, you're a good daughter. Plus, you are here now. Are you going to stay here?"

Taking a drink of wine before I answer I say, "I think so. I want to help him. He needs me, so I'll stay."

"Well, I think it's going to be tough but I'm proud of you Maddie for doing this. I don't think I would have it in me. My mother was the caretaker for her mother for several years before she passed, and I'll never forget it. It took a lot out of her. What are you going to do about your apartment?"

Crap, I have no idea. "I may just have to leave the place empty until the lease is up. It's through December though. That's going to be tough for me, but I might not have a choice."

"Well, maybe under the circumstances, you can get out of the lease. It might be worth checking anyway."

"I'm not sure; I haven't even begun to figure this entirely out yet. Maybe I can put an ad out for a temporary tenant while I am gone. I don't know how long I am going to be here though."

"You know, I have a friend at the school who is looking for his son to have somewhere to stay while he is back from college for summer. I guess their house is under renovation and they don't have the room for him right now. Do you want me to check with him?"

"That would be great, thank you Min."

"Oh, by the way, I put your mail in my bag. You will want to call the post office and have a forward set up."

"Yeah, that's at the top of my list. Can I grab it out of your bag?"

"Sure, go ahead."

I race over to her bag that is in the spare bedroom and rummage through the mail she brought. Bills, more bills, junk mail, and then finally I spot a letter from Jonah. If a heart could smile, mine would. I open it to read it quickly.

Maddie – knowing that someone out there, someone on the outside is missing me, brings me more peace than I can even say. Thank you for that. I think it goes without saying but I miss you too. Spending time with you was the best part of my week. To get back to your letter and answer your questions, I never really had a plan for my life. I was always too focused on the present. When you are a kid without a home, you find yourself just taking it day by day. I have always liked losing myself in a good book though. They were hard to come by growing up but when I was able to get my hands on one, I would love it. It never really mattered the type of story. As long as I could escape for a few hours from my own. If I had to say what I wish I could do, I would say I want to be a writer. I have always been envious of those who can create a world of make-believe and have the ability to transport you to another place. That is the dream.

I wish I could enjoy the warm weather without doing so in a cage. What I wouldn't give to go to the beach again. If you have the chance, go to the beach for me. I wish I had more interesting things to say, but not much happens when your life is spent in prison. Nothing new goes on. Each day is the same routine. Your letters are the only thing to break it up. Write me back when you can
– Jonah

After I finish Jonah's letter it hits me. His story about the invisible boy; maybe I could get it published. That would be an amazing way to say thank you for saving my life. That and being a character witness at his trial; I need to check with his lawyer about that tomorrow.

Thrilled by my publishing idea I run downstairs and ask Min if she knows anything about how to get something published. She sits on the back deck underneath a warm breeze and gives me a quizzical look.

I explain in a hurry, "I think I should publish the short story Jonah wrote. It is an amazing story that brought me to tears. I think it would be a nice way to thank him. What do you think?"

"Oh, Maddie if you want to you could self-publish it. I know someone who did that at work, it might cost a little bit of money if you want to pay for a professional editor, but if that's something you want to do, I could help you look into it. Can I read the story first?"

"Sure." I immediately run over to my bedroom and grab the pages out of the top of my dresser drawer.

I have it stashed there along with all of his letters and his mugshot.

"Awesome. I'll give it a read tonight and then we can

talk more about it."

~~~

Dad never comes back down after his nap and I check on him once and see he is sound asleep. He tires easily and this was a big day with Min here.

Min and I stay up late catching up, "So how's Jonah? Are you two still writing to each other?"

"He's as good as he can be considering the circumstances. And yes, we're still writing. His trial is in the fall and I'm trying not to get my hopes up about it. The warden of North Branch is going to provide character witness testimony at the trial because of what Jonah did during the riot and how he alerted the guards. I have been thinking about doing the same. For now, though, I'm just trying to focus on my dad and how I'm going to make this work with me taking care of him."

"That'd be very nice of you to be a character witness. What would that entail exactly?"

"I'm not sure; I still need to contact Jonah's lawyer and find out."

"I see, what about your plans on returning to school? Are you going to be able to do that if you are taking care of your dad?"

"Well, once I hear back from the two places I applied to, it might make the most sense for me to do the program offered at Walden University because I can do that online. It would be tough for me to care for dad and go to school even if it is online because taking care of him is feeling more like a full-time job. But I think I could do it."

"I know you can Maddie. You have always been one of the most motivated and diligent people I know."

After a few minutes, Min asks the question she has been waiting to ask, "What if he does get out of prison Maddie? What then?"

I mull over her question before I answer, "I don't know." It is the truth. "I guess I will deal with that if it happens. I can't worry about it too much right now." I say this hoping she will drop it.

"Okay, Maddie. I just want you to be careful."

"Thanks, I know. That's enough about my garbage can of a life. What about you? How is Raymond?"

We stay up talking for another hour and I am so glad she came to visit. I needed this more than I ever knew.

Chapter Twenty-Seven

As time goes on, I start to get into a routine with dad. While some days are better than others are, it is nice to be around him this much, even when he is having a bad day. We talk about a lot when he can, and he constantly reminds me how wise he is. He shares stories I had never heard before from his childhood and he talks a lot about mom. I am becoming more and more grateful for this time with him.

It takes me a while before I get a chance to write Jonah back. I want to tell him everything that is going on but by the time I get around to trying to write to him, I find that I am too tired and fall asleep with my pen in hand.

Finally, one day while dad is napping, I take a moment to write.

Jonah- I am sorry this letter is coming later than normal. I have so much going on and so much to tell you. I ended up having to move back home with my dad in Frederick, Maryland. He has Huntington's disease and requires full-time care. I figured that since I no longer have a full-time job, it would make the most sense if I took on caring for him. He is stubborn and would not listen to a stranger anyway. It is a lot of work, but I am happy to do it. I love spending this time with him. It has been tough seeing my dad decline so much. He is a great man and the only family I have left. My mother died a while ago. I don't have any sisters or brothers. Soon my father will pass, and I won't have any family. It is hard for me to think about. I am not ready to lose him. I get an overwhelming feeling of dread just thinking about it.

I wanted to let you know that I am working on a couple of projects for you as a way to say thank you for saving me that day, but I don't want to tell you about them yet. Not until I am sure I can get them completed. By the way, I have told my best friend Min about you. About our letters and how I feel about you. She is great; I think you would like her. I have included with this letter some lavender from the garden. I have dried and flattened it in a book, but it still has that wonderful lavender smell. I figured that since you can't enjoy the summer, maybe I would bring some summer to you. Also, I love the beach as well. I might try to see if dad is up for taking a day trip to the coast. I think the fresh ocean air might be good for him. I will send you some sand if we do go. Do write me back, even if you don't have anything new to say, just say anything. – Maddie

I fold the letter and place it in an envelope when my phone rings. It is Min.

"I loved the story Jonah wrote Maddie. The cost to publish is free, but we need to pay for a cover and a professional editing service. What do you think?"

"I am on board, let's do it. Text me the amount and I'll send you the money."

After we get off the phone, I open up my computer to search Mark Wessley, the lawyer whose name I wrote down during one of my meetings with Jonah. I do a quick search, find his law office and email, and shoot him a quick email asking if the case could benefit from having another character witness. I hope these gestures will show Jonah just how grateful I am for what he did for me.

Chapter Twenty-Eight

The weather is threatening to change with a slight crisp in the breeze. It is now mid-August and I think it is a good time to take dad on a trip to the beach before it gets too cold. He is not scheduled for physical therapy for the next two days and he is thrilled to get out of the house and go somewhere besides the doctor's office.

Ocean City is right on the coast and is about three hours away from Frederick. We head in that direction without evening discussing it; there is no need to. Ocean City is the spot we used to go with mom when I was a kid. Those are some of my, and I suspect my dad's, favorite memories. I remember building sandcastles with mom, and dad's laughter playing like music in the background. The image of the orange and red, painting the sky as the sun went down; our sandcastle masterpiece on full display while we snuggled under a blanket together; makes me smile even in the worst of times.

The windows are down as we sing along to the radio. I look over to dad, his crow's feet are emphasized by his wide smile. The wind whips through our hair and the music flows through the air between us.

At the beach, we set up a spot with a blanket, finding an area with the cleanest sand and the best view. With a lunch basket and thermoses of tea, we are well on our way to a perfect day. It is still a bit chilly by the coast, which I anticipated, so I pull out our hoodies and extra blankets.

We sit silently, bundled up under the clear blue sky, watching waves slowly coming and going. The salty ocean breeze fills up my lungs and I smile.

Munching on a roast beef sandwich I packed the night before dad asks, "So what has been going on with you Maddie?"

Casually I inquire, "What do you mean dad?"

"Well, we have talked about a lot of things since you got home, mostly about my health, but we have yet to talk about you. I can tell that you lost your job or quit, or you wouldn't be able to be here taking care of me. So, what is going on with you? What happened?"

Okay, it is truth time.

"It's a long story dad," he gives me a sideways look, so I continue, "basically I made a mistake at work and it cost me."

"Oh, I see. Well without knowing the details I don't

know if I can offer you much advice."

Hesitant to talk about it I say, "It's complicated dad."

"Why don't you just tell me, Maddie? Keeping things to yourself is not healthy. You know that."

"I know dad. Fine, I will tell you but try not to pass too much judgment on me."

"Maddie you're my daughter and I love you. I just want to help," he smiles at me, providing comfort.

"Well, I was working on a research project at the North Branch Correctional Institute. We were researching violent criminals when I met an inmate named Jonah. I don't know what else to say other than I did the worst thing I could do, I developed feelings for him, dad. I know that sounds crazy, but he ended up not being what I thought and for lack of fewer cliché words, I fell in love with him."

I cannot bear to look at my father's face after I say this.

"So, did this cost you your job?"

"Well yes and no. My boss, Dr. Flanigan found out that I had continued the research with him even after he told me that he was not the type of offender we were looking to research. My ethics waned and it cost me all of it. It was a huge error on my part, so she pulled me off the project, which I understand. After I lost my job, I went to the prison to tell him in person that I could not continue the research anymore. If I am being honest, it was really to see him one more time, and that is when the riot broke out. He saved my life dad. If he hadn't done what he did that day, I don't think I would be here talking to you now."

I stop to catch a breath for a moment before saying, "I guess that sums it up."

I muster up the courage to look at him. As expected, he looks shocked. It takes him a while to recover.

"You are in love with a convict who saved your life during a prison riot?"

"Yes, dad."

"Are you in touch with this person?"

"We write to each other."

"Jesus Maddie, what has gotten into you?"

"This is why I didn't want to tell you, dad," I say, sounding exacerbated.

"Sorry Maddie, but that was not at all what I was expecting. I don't know what to say. It's just so unlike you. How are you planning to have a relationship with someone in prison? Is there a chance he could get out?"

"He was sentenced to thirty-eight years. I'm not planning to have a relationship with him. It's not possible so I have settled on us being pen pals. With his case going to a retrial, there is a chance he could get a reduced sentence, but it would still probably be for many years so I'm not counting on it."

Dad goes quiet and seems to be contemplating. His eyebrows scrunch the way they always are when he is concerned.

After what seems like a lifetime he says, "Maddie, not to sound judgmental, but do you think you might be looking for love in all the wrong places?"

"Yes, I've thought that Dad. I truly don't know what I am doing. Any advice you have I would like to hear."

"Maddie, I'm no expert on love or relationships. Your mother and I had a wonderful and successful relationship, but I credit your mother with most of that. You know there is a quote by Atticus that I heard your mother say more than once, maybe if she were here, she would say it now."

"What is it, dad?"

"Okay it goes, 'never go in search of love, go in search

of life, and life will find you the love you seek.' Have you heard that before Maddie?"

I think for a second then respond, "Yeah actually. I remember mom saying that before, but I never understood it. What does it mean?"

Dad shrugs, "Maddie, you are one of the smartest people I know. You've always made good decisions. You're levelheaded but, falling in love with some convict and losing your job is not you and it's not smart. I don't know what is going on with you, but I would advise you to focus on living your life and finding joy instead of worrying about this relationship, just like the quote suggests."

"How do I do that?"

"Well, you have never really let yourself live, you've always been so tightly wound. Instead of worrying, live Maddie, I mean are you happy?"

I turn to him stunned, "I'm not happy. I have been feeling like I am just going through the motions for some time now, never really living but just existing."

Dad offers me a genuine smile and I bite my lip to hold back tears.

"I have felt like I have lost my mind since the divorce

and this project at work. My life has completely fallen apart, and I am trying to pick up the pieces and figure out what I want. It's as if I am starting over and I'm terrified. My entire life plan has collapsed, and I don't know what to do about it . . . then this riot happened, and it shocked me to my core. I want to change my life, take advantage of this second chance but I don't know how . . . What would mom do?"

Dad sets down his thermos of tea; smooshing the sand around to make it more secure, "Maddie, life is hard. You have had it easy up until your divorce other than losing your mother. You were always one to plan everything. Maybe that is the problem. Maybe you are trying too hard to develop a plan. Maybe it is time to go with where the wind takes you."

I smile, "Thank you, dad. It is nice to talk about it. However, I am not so sure that is what mom would do."

He looks surprised and says, "What do you mean Maddie?"

"Dad, mom planned for everything. She was the most prepared person I have ever met. She would never go 'where the wind takes her'."

"Oh Maddie, you misunderstand your mother. You

don't know this but at the end of her life, in the last few months, she told me she regretted not living more spontaneously. She had regrets, Maddie. She never allowed herself to be free. She always dreamed of traveling the world like we talked about when we were young but never did, we never did because there was always something else going on, something that we thought required our total focus. First with our careers and later with you. However, she regretted it, not you of course, but of not traveling. She was worried she made you the same way. She hoped you would learn to let go of plans and live in the moment . . . I'm sorry Maddie I never told you that, I wanted to, but I didn't know how. I guess I didn't want you to know that your mother died with regrets. But then maybe we all die with some regrets."

Shocked I say quickly, "She died with regrets dad? She always seemed so content and happy to me. I thought she died satisfied with her life, other than it being cut short."

My heart is aching, "Yes she had regrets, Maddie. She wanted to always seem happy and content because she didn't like to show you any sadness. Especially when she found out about the cancer, she didn't want to make it harder on you by being sad, but she wished she had lived her life differently."

He pauses, "Oh, don't get me wrong Maddie, she wouldn't trade you or myself for anything, but she wished she had learned how to enjoy the time she had more. She spent too much of her time worrying and planning for things. I don't want you to make the same mistakes. Life is short; please stop trying to follow some life plan. Do it for her. Hell, travel as she always wanted to. I have a box full of travel guides and inspiration your mother collected for years, you can have it. Maddie, I don't think I have much time left on this earth, I don't want to go worrying about you. Please learn to embrace your life, it passes by so fast. Do me a favor and promise me you will travel to at least one city outside of the U.S. Go there on a whim, without planning every detail, and stay there for some time; at least for a month and go alone. Please take my advice, do it for your mother, do it for me."

Shaken, I simply nod, wishing more than ever that I could talk to my mom.

Chapter Twenty-Nine

That day at the beach ends up being the last good day I had with my dad. Now his memory and body have deteriorated to the point that he is rarely able to leave his bed; continually reminding me about how fragile life is. The doctor's say he does not have much time left and recommend that I have hospice come in once a day and assist.

How could this be? He cannot leave me so soon. I want more time with him, we were just beginning to break down the barriers of our relationship and grow close.

Hospice comes in and sets up a hospital bed in our living room along with an IV that administers a stream of pain medication. When he is able, he reads. It has always been his favorite hobby.

It is a brisk Thursday afternoon as I make my way to the mailbox; I see a letter from Jonah and two letters from both universities I have applied. I tear them open quickly and see that they are both acceptance letters and the programs begin in the spring. I am uncertain if dad will still be alive in the spring so I do not think I can commit to either program. I want to be present full time for dad.

I read the letter from Jonah and it provides me with a break from the sadness around me, albeit brief.

Maddie – It sounds like you are going through a lot. I am so sorry to hear about your dad. I wish I could be there in person to comfort you. I feel so helpless. How much time does he have left? When I read your letter, I thought of a story. I wrote it for you and I included it here. I hope that it makes you smile and brings you some peace. Thank you for the flowers. You are right; they still had a fragrance to them. I have them taped on the cell wall next to your picture. I am made fun of for it, but I don't mind. I don't know what it is that you are trying to work on for me, but I hope you know it's not necessary. You do not need to worry about doing anything for me. Especially with everything you have going on. You said in your letter that you told your friend Min about how you feel about me. How do you feel about me, Maddie? I know you are grateful that I was able to help you during the riot, but is that it? Are your feelings towards me that of gratitude, friendship? We have only kissed twice so I don't want to get ahead of myself, but I want you to know that you are the only brightness in my life. Also, while I love getting your letters, know that you don't need to feel bad if you aren't able to write for a while because of all you have going on in your life. I will understand. Just know that I am here, thinking of you. – Jonah

The short story Jonah sent me is two pages long and titled *The Lonely Dove*. It is about a white dove that goes through life with another dove, her dad. The two do everything together and are inseparable. The father knows that his time has come to pass on, but he worries his daughter will be too sad without him. Therefore, he devises a plan to live forever. He eats a magic plant that gives him eternal life. His daughter ends up spending all of her time with her father. Then one day, her father notices a family of doves, with a mother and father dove and baby doves by their side. He looks to his daughter and realizes that she has not been able to start a family of her own because she is never away from her father long enough to meet a male dove to start a family with. It dawns on him that by never leaving her side, he is preventing her from creating a life of her own. With that, he sneaks away one night while she sleeps and never returns. She assumes he has died and grieves. Over time, however, she begins to heal and one day she meets a nice dove who wants to start a family with her. She goes on to great happiness raising her baby doves and living with her family. She is not aware, but the entire time she lives her life, her father is high up on a cliff watching over her. He is smiling down, feeling happy about what he has given her.

I cry as I read and reread the ending, pondering about death and the afterlife. I regret not spending more time with dad when he was healthy; life is so unfair. While I have never been a religious person, I have a hope that somewhere, somehow, after dad passes, he will join mom and will be watching over me.

~~~

Time has no concept as each day blends; I sit by my father's side, holding his hand and reading to him as the seconds keep passing by. Dad has no mobility left and his cognition continues to break down as he struggles to remember most things. The caregivers from hospice are now at the house every four hours, assisting with bodily functions and pain administration.

It is now the end of September and Jonah's trial is fast is approaching. I have exchanged a few emails with Mark Wessley, and I am supposed to be a character witness, but I am scared to leave dad's side. I have developed a fear that he will pass away, and I will not be there for him.

I call Min seeking reassurance, "Min, I'm worried about leaving my dad to go to Jonah's trial. What would you do?"

"Maddie, I'm going to be honest, I wouldn't leave. I'd be too worried that something would happen while I was away."

"Maybe you are right, maybe I should cancel, but I already promised to be there, and I may not get another chance to see Jonah again."

"Well, it sounds like you have already decided what you are going to do. I can come up and be with your dad while you away, but I would think about this Maddie."

"You would come up and stay with him Min? That would be wonderful, thank you so much. You are truly the best friend a girl could have," I say, ignoring her advice.

Min tries to lighten my worry by saying, "I know I'm the best friend you could have, don't forget it," but does not offer the reassurance I was seeking.

She goes on to tell me that it is official; Jonah's short story is published online. She put it through the professional editing process, and they created a cover for it. With everything going on, I have not been able to respond to Jonah's last letter. Instead of writing, I will tell him at the trial about his short story being published. It is something I would like to share with him in person.

Mark Wessley calls me one afternoon to make sure that I will be at the trial. "Ms. Tilltot, I want to thank you for asking to provide character witness testimony. It is not often that I work with a client with multiple people requesting to provide such testimony. The trial will probably last a few days so pack enough clothes to last a week."

Leaving dad for an entire week seems impossible so, I do not say it to Mark but plan to leave after two days regardless of how the trial is progressing.

When the day finally arrives, I say goodbye to dad, every molecule of my body begging for this to not be the last time I see him alive, "Dad, I have to go away for a couple of days. Please hold on until I get back. I want to be here with you as much as I can. You won't be alone though; Min is going to be here. I love you."

Min says, "Hurry back Maddie," but I hear it in dad's voice.

Chapter Thirty

The morning of the trial, I meet with Mark at a local coffee shop to review everything that he wants me to discuss. He hits me with questions that he believes the prosecution is likely to ask me upon cross-examination.

Mark is optimistic, "I hope that Jonah will get a much lighter sentence in light of his character which is apparent, thanks to the heroic actions he took on the day of the riot to save you and potentially many more. I don't think he will get off the hook completely because he did commit the home invasion, but I am really trying to get the jury to see that he is not a violent offender and did not assault anyone, therefore should not be convicted on that charge. His accomplice Zeek will be called to testify about Jonah's role in the robbery. That may end up being the key to this case. Also, I don't know if you know this, but the warden of North Branch is also going to testify on his behalf as a character witness."

I nod, "Yes, I did know that. That is how I came up with the idea to do the same."

Mark explains further, "The purpose of you and the warden is to discuss situations in which the defendant demonstrated honesty, trustworthiness, and accountability. I believe that is clear with his actions during the riot. I think it will show that he is not the type of person to assault anyone and that he is being honest when he says he fled the scene. We'll see though."

Mark continues to explain that he was able to get a retrial because a trial court granted his motion on the grounds of a technicality that occurred during the first trial. Apparently, evidence was not disclosed during the first trial. The evidence was that of the interrogation tapes of Zeek and Jonah.

Additionally, the cops lied, "They knew that Jonah had not assaulted anyone and had fled the scene and while I was searching through all of the interrogation tapes on Jonah and Zeek, Zeek told them repeatedly that he acted alone, and that Jonah did not hurt anyone. For some reason, the cops decided to leave this part out of their write up and Jonah's original defense attorney did not bother to review the tapes in their entirety. He had the worst defense attorney."

Mark is going to approach the jury with the truth about what is said on the tapes, he is also going to play a large portion of the tapes for the jury to see and hear for themselves Zeek's version of the assault. Mark is going to do something unusual and put Jonah on the stand as well.

It is a risky move, "Some might think I am crazy for having Jonah testify in his own defense, but he has such a likable face, I think it'll help his case."

He explains, "The length of sentence in the state of Maryland for armed robbery is twenty years for the maximum. Jonah is currently serving thirty-eight because of the additional charge of criminal assault. I think the sentence needs to be twenty years or less, well much less. I worked on a case recently, that was similar to Jonah's and ended with a fifty-one-month sentence. This demonstrates just how much the length of the sentence can vary."

"Did you tell him that I was going to serve as a character witness?"

"Yes, I did just yesterday. He seemed surprised but grateful."

I am nervous about seeing Jonah, but I am more nervous for him. I cannot imagine how he must be feeling about all of this.

~~~

The trial starts at ten in the morning and we all funnel into the courtroom. I sit in the back; I do not want to be a distraction for Jonah.

Jonah is escorted into the courtroom; he is dressed in a dark suit with a pinstriped blue and gray tie.

Damn, he looks good.

His hair is cut and is no longer the floppy look I had grown accustomed to. With the suit, haircut, and clean-shaven face, he is beautiful, but he also looks very young and it startles me for a moment. He quickly scans the room before taking his place by Mark.

The judge comes in and we all rise.

The trial begins.

The prosecution goes first, and Mark tells me during a brief intermission that they regurgitated almost the same argument from the first trial. During the first trial, the defense attorney never asked an important question of the homeowners: did one person or two assault you? The homeowners, a husband and wife, both say that only one person physically attacked them when police interviewed them. They also said they could not identify which man attacked them because the man was wearing a mask and was careful not to say much to them, in an attempt to conceal his identity. Mark plans to ask these crucial questions.

As the trial continues, Mark is most excited about a piece of information that the male homeowner reveals during questioning that did not come out during the first trial. The homeowner testified that before the one assailant fled the scene, he first said to the other assailant something to the effect of, "What the hell man, you told me no one is home! We can't do this!" This information further corroborates Jonah's version of what happened and conflicts with what the police originally stated had happened. The homeowners also do not recall both assailants having a weapon. They know one did, but they could not say for sure if the other assailant did.

The cops who worked the case originally are called to testify by the prosecution. Upon cross-examination, Mark is successful in getting them to admit that they could not prove that both men assaulted the victims.

The first part of the trial was already not looking good for the prosecution.

The prosecution's side went on all day and the judge said the case would reconvene the next morning.

I get up to leave the courtroom when Jonah spots me.

It must have been for the first time based on the look on his face. He was careful not to give too much away but I could still feel the intensity. His eyes light up and a small, half-smile comes across his face. I blush and smile back, trying to keep it subtle, but I fail and Mark notices it immediately. By the look on his face, I can tell he is not happy as he walks toward the back of the room to speak with me.

"Madeline, can I speak to you privately?"

"Of Course, Mark," I say as we make our way out of the courtroom and out of earshot.

"Uh, Madeline, is your relationship with Jonah strictly professional or . . .?"

"You know I write to him Mark, I told you that."

"I thought you wrote to him just to tell him to thank you and you didn't answer my question."

I hesitate, "Well, we don't have a sexual relationship Mark."

"That's not what I'm asking Madeline and you know it."

"Okay, okay, I know. We do write to each other. They are harmless letters. I mean we are attracted to each other, but I wouldn't call it a relationship."

"Ugh Madeline, don't you understand? The prosecution will have a field day if they learn that. They will ruin your credibility as a character witness upon cross-examination."

Panicked I respond, "I don't see how they could know that Mark."

Mark's eyes are big as he says, "There are a lot of ways they can learn that kind of information."

"I understand what you are saying and I'm sorry I was not more upfront with our relationship Mark. Do you still want to use me as a character witness?"

Mark sighs before saying, "Yes I do. Let's just hope the prosecution does not know about it."

"Okay, Mark. Again, I'm sorry."

"Let's just forget it and I will see you tomorrow Madeline."

Dejected, I say, "Okay."

~~~

That night in my hotel room, I call Min to check on dad.

"He's doing okay Maddie; I have to say that I can't believe you are doing this every day. It's so hard."

"I know it is. Thanks so much for doing this for me

Min. Has he been asking for me?" I say, hoping he has missed me.

"Yes, he has, he keeps forgetting where you went but I keep reminding him that you will be back soon."

"Oh man, well thanks again for doing this for me, I can't tell you how much I appreciate this."

"I'm happy to help Maddie, I love your dad."

"I know you do."

"How's the trial going?"

I pause before saying, "It's going well. I think Jonah has a chance at getting a much lighter sentence. I'm stressed though because Mark worries that my relationship with Jonah will hurt my credibility as a character witness."

"Does he know that you lost your job, Maddie?"

I pause, "No he doesn't. Do you think I should tell him?"

"Yes, if the prosecution knows, I would think they would also use that against you."

Despondent I say, "Yeah, you're right. I will call Mark now and talk with him. Please put dad on the phone so I can tell him goodnight."

After I get off the phone with dad, I call and talk with

Mark. I am honest about everything that happened with my job at the F.B.I. and I can tell he is tense.

"Okay, the good news is that unless the prosecution found someone willing to talk then it shouldn't come up. I assume that the F.B.I. maintains very strict confidentiality regarding that type of stuff. Do you think anyone would rat you out like that if they were approached?"

At that moment, Dave flashes in my mind but I push it aside. Surely, he would not do that to me; he would be risking his own job if he did.

"Nobody I can think of Mark."

"Okay let's not worry about it then and hope for the best. Depending on time, I expect to call on you tomorrow so make sure you are wearing your most professional-looking outfit."

I roll my eyes; of course, I will look professional, "Will do Mark, see you then."

That night I cannot sleep. I replay every scenario I can think of repeatedly in my mind. Eventually, I give up and write Jonah a letter instead:

Jonah - I am writing you this the day before I am to be

a character witness at your trial. I am sick with nerves. I want to help you so much. I have tried to put this trial out of my head, I have tried not to get my hopes up about you getting out of prison, but I find the image of you drifting into my mind when I least expect it. No matter how hard I try to force myself to not care about you, I am unsuccessful. You asked me in your last letter how I feel about you. It is scary for me to say this because I am not used to letting my guard down, but I want you to know that I think I am in love with you. I honestly think I have been ever since I first laid eyes on you. I know that seems crazy, but I want you to know. You deserve to know. You saved my life and all I want to do is save yours. I hope that my testimony will help you but if it doesn't, if you end up spending the rest of your life in prison, I want you to know that your life was not wasted. I have felt your impact. I am grateful to know you and even if I never get to interact with you outside of prison walls, I will cherish knowing you. Thank you, for everything – Maddie

Chapter Thirty-One

The next day I put on a black, long-sleeved blazer with a white blouse underneath. I have black trousers and flats and I opt for no jewelry and minimal makeup. At the last second, I change out my contacts for my black-rimmed glasses. My hair is pulled back into a bun, I could not look more professional.

Trying not to sound forced, I walk up to Mark and say, "I got this."

He appears reassured as we proceed inside the courtroom. I take a seat in the same spot from yesterday and peek over to Jonah. He is in a light gray suit with a solid blue tie. I am curious as to where he got the clothes but then realize they are probably from Mark. An article posted online about his trial this morning describes him as *The Beautiful Bandit.* Apparently, I am not the only person who has noticed his good looks and I feel a ping of jealously over not being able to keep him all to myself.

The trial begins with an opening statement from Mark. His approach is simple. It is direct and honest. He states, "Jonah did burglarize the home and he should be punished for his crime, but he should not be convicted of assault charges because he never assaulted anybody. By the end of this trail, you, the jury, will see that. Jonah is not violent at all and his true character will come to light."

He starts by going through the details of the crime and by playing the interrogation tapes from when Zeek and Jonah were first arrested.

The jury, and everyone else in the courtroom, sit on the edges of their seats as they hear Zeek on tape, "Jonah did not hurt those people I did. He wouldn't do that."

Next, they hear Jonah, "I never hurt anybody. I don't know what Zeek did; I had already run off before I saw anything."

Mark calls on Zeek to testify. While he was not a very credible witness, Mark is happy that Zeek corroborates Jonah's version by stating that he lied to Jonah about the homeowners being gone because he needed another set of hands to help him at the scene and he knew Jonah would not help if he knew the homeowners were home.

Finally, it is time for the first character witness, the warden of North Branch Correctional Institution. The warden explains what happened at the North Branch Correctional facility on the day of the riot. He explains that Jonah can be seen on tape, rescuing an F.B.I. researcher from being attacked by four other inmates.

"Jonah M. tipped off the guards to the riot, thereby possibly preventing an even worse situation. He did not have to do this. In fact, by doing so, he made himself enemy number one at North Branch, forcing us to have him relocated to another facility in another state so he could be safe. Jonah's actions surprised me so much so, I was compelled to speak on behalf of his character."

With this, the prosecution chooses not to cross-examine. The warden is a very credible witness, and they know it.

Then comes my turn.

My name is called so I get up and walk down the center aisle of the courtroom.

Every eye in the room is on me and time seems to slow down.

My body breaks out in goosebumps and my heart is pounding against my chest, threatening to break the very shell that is keeping me together.

"You can do this," I reassure myself in a hushed whisper.

I swear in and Mark starts by asking me the exact

questions we talked about previously and I answer them the way we practiced.

I explain, "I was at the prison researching for the F.B.I. when the riot broke out and if it wasn't for Jonah M. I could have been killed. He truly saved my life."

"Ms. Tilltot, through your work with the defendant, in your professional opinion, is he a violent man? Capable of hurting anyone?"

"In my professional opinion, no he is not."

"Is that not why you had to pull the work you did with the defendant from your research project? Because he was not violent enough?"

"Yes, that is true." Kind of. The weight of being under oath begins to sit on my chest.

The questioning from Mark appears to go well and I mistakenly begin to relax a bit. The prosecutor, a man named Terry Burton, who reminds me of a bulldog, is up to cross-examine me. Even though I rehearsed with Mark and ran through many scenarios in my head, I am not prepared for Terry's questions.

"Ms. Tilltot, is it true you were fired from your position at the F.B.I.?"

Shocked, Mark jumps in, "Objection, relevancy."

Terry is prepared, "Trust me your honor it is going somewhere."

The Judge says, "Overruled."

Looking pleased, Terry says to me, "Answer the question Ms. Tilltot."

I am stunned and instantly regret doing this, "Uh, yes I was let go from my position."

"And is it true that you were fired due to having poor judgment?" My mouth drops open as I look to Mark who looks just as shocked as I do.

I shift in my seat, "I was removed from the research project because I did not make a good call on what to do about a certain situation." It is the truth.

"Ms. Tilltot, I have spoken with a credible source that you worked with at the F.B.I. and he says that you had terrible judgment and he went on to say that you broke F.B.I. protocol by getting *involved* with one of the inmates at the prison that you were researching on, is that correct?"

The word lingers in the air, *involved*.

Dave.

"I did not get involved with anyone Mr. Burton."

"Really? You don't send romantic letters to this man

still to this day?" He says as he points to Jonah.

Gasps are audible.

Oh no.

"I have a pen pal but that is not illegal."

"No, but it is not ethical in your line of work is it?"

Mark has had enough, "Objection! Leading!"

"Sustained."

"Fine your honor. Okay, Ms. Tilltot, are you in a romantic relationship with the defendant?"

Jonah's eyes are huge, mouth agape.

"No, it is a friendship."

"Why did you send him a picture of yourself then Ms. Tilltot?"

"Objection! Leading!" shouts Mark.

"Withdrawn your honor."

With that, the cross-examination is done, and I leave the stand. I cannot bring myself to make eye contact with Jonah.

Horror in the form of embarrassment fills every pore on my skin, coating me in a layer of regret.

I should not have come here.

~~~

The judge calls a brief intermission, and my face is hot.

I expect Mark to come over to me and yell at me but instead, he surprises me, "It's okay Madeline, I still think we got this."

"You don't think I have ruined this for him?"

"Oh no, my arguments still stand and the Warden as a character witness was solid. Your statements should not negatively impact the outcome."

Relieved I say, "Thanks, Mark. I'm so embarrassed."

"I know Madeline, but don't leave okay? I know Jonah wants you here for the rest of the trial."

My heart swells, "Okay, I want to be here for him."

I head to the bathroom and splash water on my face, trying to cool off the heat from embarrassment. I notice another woman to my right washing her hands. She is wearing a leopard print tank top and her red bra strap is falling down her shoulder, her unkempt hair has me questioning if she is homeless. She is so quiet that when she turns to speak to me, I barely register it at first.

"Excuse me? I saw you on the stand. Do you have a relationship with Jonah?"

The question does not offend me, after what just

happened, I should expect it.

By her attire, I doubt she is a reporter, and she looks too old to be a former lover, "Well, kind of. We are pen pals. Why do you ask?" I am trying not to sound rude.

"I see. Well just so you know he has had a hard life. His parents were deep into drugs and it impacted him."

My interest is peaked, "I'm sorry, I haven't introduced myself, my name is Madeline Tilltot, and you are . . .?"

"Oh, I'm sorry, my name is Lisa Molloy. I'm Jonah's aunt. His mother was my sister. She died a long time ago."

A family member, I was not expecting this, "I'm sorry to hear that. Have you been involved in Jonah's life much?"

"Not as much as I should've been. When his mother died, I was a struggling single mother of two little kids. I worked as a server and just didn't have enough money to take on another kid. He ended up having to go into foster care and I have regretted it ever since. He doesn't know I am here today. I just had to come. I hope to make amends with him. I blame myself for a lot of this."

"Well, you're here now and that's something," I say genuinely trying to comfort Lisa who seems distraught.

"Thank you, Madeline, I appreciate that. I just hope he still wants me in his life. See you inside?"

I leave the bathroom and sit in a chair outside of the courtroom; I take several deep breaths, too embarrassed to go back inside. I use this time to call Dr. Flanigan. I want to report that I suspect Dave breached confidentiality and leaked my term information to Terry Burton; but as I begin to, I change my mind and hang up my phone. It dawns on me that blaming Dave and seeking revenge against him is not the right thing to do. It is not his fault that I got fired, it is not his fault that Terry Burton found out about my conduct, it is not his fault that I am sitting here in embarrassment. There is only one person to blame for my actions: me. It is a painful, stark realization, gripping my chest.

~~~

After intermission, Mark calls on Jonah to testify on his own behalf and Mark hopes *The Beautiful Bandit* will sway the jury.

As his name is called, there is a rustling among the jurors and the crowd. Jonah is escorted over to standby a guard; his suit and tie are in stark contrast to the handcuffs around his wrists and the shackles around his ankles. After he vows to tell the truth, he sits down, and Mark gets to work.

"Jonah, can you tell me what happened on the night of June tenth?"

Jonah sits straight as he responds, "Yes. I was staying at a friend's place when Zeek came by around ten p.m. He told me that he knows of an empty home he wants to hit. He said he needs my help. We break in through a window to the basement, I start gathering the electronics in the living room. After only a few minutes, a man comes down the stairs in his robe. Zeek jumps him and ties him up as the wife comes down the stairs. Zeek ties them both up. I tell Zeek we need to run. I try to convince him to leave but Zeek wants to finish the hit. I didn't want to hurt the homeowners or finish the hit, so I fled out the back door."

Mark jumps in at this point, "Jonah, did you know the homeowners were home?"

"No sir."

"Would you have gone to the home if you knew?"

"No sir."

"Did you assault the homeowners?"

"No sir."

"Do you have anything you want to say about what happened that night?"

Jonah sighs and says, "Yes. I want to say that I am sorry. I am sorry to the homeowners for everything that happened. I hope they can forgive me one day."

Mark keeps the questions brief before it's turned over to the prosecution. Terry is unprepared to cross-examine Jonah, as I am sure he never expected he would be called on to testify in his own defense. Terry's cross-examination is brief and does not yield much benefit. The trial ends with closing statements from both Mark and the prosecutor.

Terry argues, "Jonah should be sentenced to the maximum. He is a dangerous criminal and will commit more crimes if he is released."

Mark argues, "The prosecution could not prove that Jonah was violent and while he has made some major mistakes, he should not be sentenced to the maximum amount of time and he should not be convicted of assault because I have proved to you that Jonah did not assault the victims."

I watch Jonah throughout closing arguments and he does not give much away. He is calm and collected, with a hint of sadness. His aunt Lisa sits behind him in the back, out of view from Jonah. The judge gives the jury instruction, and they break to deliberate. After two hours, the jury comes back with a verdict.

Jonah is found guilty of the home invasion charge but is found not guilty of the assault charge. The judge sentences Jonah to a sixty-month prison term with time served. Jonah has already served his time meaning that he is now a free man.

Elation prevents the breath in my body from escaping; leaving me to gasp in shock.

I look to Jonah; he smiles broadly with tears in his eyes. Just as my spirit soars, a dark, heavy sensation hits my stomach and I realize that my fantasy is about to become a reality, and I am not sure I really want it to.

Chapter Thirty-Two

With court adjourned, I wait in the back of the courtroom. Jonah stands with Mark and his aunt who he embraces but, it does not take him long to make his way back to me.

"Maddie, can I hug you?" he says with a broad smile as he walks towards me.

"Of course, Jonah."

We embrace. Feeling Jonah's body against mine for the first time is unexpected in its power. I instantly relax and have the urge to cry, happy tears—tears of comfort. It is amazing how impactful a simple hug can be.

I hear Mark walk up, "I can't believe it, Madeline, can you?! I believe that the sentence now matches the crime. I just hope you learn from this Jonah and can keep out of trouble. Where are you going now that you are free?"

"My aunt asked me to stay with her for a few nights so we can catch up and I can get on my feet, so I am going to do that and then I will need to move into one of those apartments for newly released prisoners. I just can't believe this is real. I can't believe I won't be in a prison cell tonight."

Mark pats Jonah on the back and says, "Let's go grab a celebratory drink, on me."

~~~

A surprisingly refreshing evening filled with drinks and laughter brings a lightness to my heart that I have not felt in years. Seeing Jonah in normal clothes outside of those prison walls is strange and a bit unnerving.

Throughout the night, I steal glimpses of him and he of me, but I am careful to keep my distance. I was not prepared for this.

After a couple of drinks, we drop Jonah and his aunt off at her car and he asks, "Can I talk to you a moment?"

We walk to the side of the car, out of earshot, before he says quietly, "Maddie, all I want to do is spend the night with you, but I figured it was too soon for something like that and I didn't want to press my luck."

I place my hand on his chest and slide in close enough where our bodies are touching, "You're right Jonah, it is too soon for something like that. You need to figure out how to be a free man before you can jump into anything more with me. Let's take the physical stuff slowly."

The dark, heavy weight in my stomach is screaming, "Something's not right."

I grab the letter I wrote to him the night before out of my purse and give it to him. "I wrote this last night. I want you to have it, but you don't have to worry about responding to it if you are not sure how to."

Jonah's eyes are bright as he says, "Can I read it now?"

"No, I'm too embarrassed, read it later please."

Jonah puts the note in his back pocket, the light from streetlight gliding over his features; persuading me to touch him.

I place my hand on his cheek and we lock eyes, I should feel bliss but instead all I can think is that I want to go home.

"Jonah, I wanted to tell you thank you for saving me. So, I tried, and failed, to be a character witness for you,"

"Thank you so much for that Maddie, I'm so sorry that it did not go well," Jonah says, interrupting me.

"It's not your fault. Let's just pretend that it never happened, okay?"

"Done."

"I also decided to publish your short story that you gave me about the invisible boy. I have self-published it through Amazon. It's not much, but I was hoping you would appreciate the gesture since you always wanted to be a writer."

"Really? Thank you so much, Maddie. That's so sweet of you."

Jonah's hand is on the small of my back, pulling me closer to him. We lock lips and I melt into him, desperately trying to ignore the growing uncertainty.

Chapter Thirty-Three

I drive home early; pondering how much my life has changed as the fall air flows into my car. With the windows rolled down, autumn is on full display; the sun is peaking over the horizon, as the day is unfolding, waking up the world around me.

My phone ringing interrupts my contemplation. This cannot be good as I rarely get a call this early in the morning. I hold my breath before I answer, seeing that it is Min.

"Min what is it? Is dad okay?"

"Maddie, the paramedics just took him, he has stopped breathing." No.

"WHAT?"

"How quickly can you get to Frederick Memorial?"

"I'm only about thirty minutes away,"

"I'll meet you there Maddie, hurry."

~~~

The next few hours are a blur as I sit in the waiting room of Frederick Memorial, gripping the chair as I wait for word on dad. Min's words when I left for the trial, "hurry Maddie," rattling against my skull as guilt and fear grip my heart. Min does her best to comfort me by rubbing my back. A stout, concerned-looking doctor comes through the double doors, calling my name.

"Madeline?"

"YES," I say practically flying out of my seat, "is he alive?"

"Yes, Ms. Please come back with me so we can talk."

I follow the white lab coat through the bright halls until finally arriving at a dreary-looking room under a sign reading Intensive Care Unit.

"I am afraid I have some bad news. Your father is stable, but he has slipped into a coma. I do not anticipate him waking up from this. His body has deteriorated to a point where the machines are what's keeping him alive, he is no longer able to breathe on his own."

"What do you mean doctor? Are you saying I will never get to speak to him again?"

"I am so sorry Ms."

"Can I see him, please?"

"Right in here."

The man in the white lab coat motions me towards a door with the number 314 on a plaque to the side. I turn the knob and open the door slowly, trying to somehow prepare myself for what I am about to see. The room is bright with the sun filtering in through the blinds, a person is lying in the bed with numerous machines hooked up to monitors displaying information that I do not understand. As I get closer, I see dad's face. He does not look like himself, his jaw is tight, and he looks pained.

I collapse on the floor beside him, with tears flowing hard and fast, I am unable to make a sound.

Chapter Thirty-Four

I am not a selfish person.

I used to believe that.

It takes a while for Min to tell me about my father's last moments awake, and when she finally does, my worst fears are realized.

"Maddie, he called out, asking for you, it startled me awake and by the time I ran down the stairs and got to him, he wasn't breathing anymore. He was turning a bluish color and I called 911. I'm so sorry I couldn't do anything for him."

He called out for me in his last moments and I was not there. The shame and guilt fill my body. "Min, you've nothing to apologize for. It's not your fault that I wasn't there. I didn't want this to be the end. I thought I had more time. I thought I could say goodbye and be by his side as he slipped away. I can't believe I wasn't there for him. I can't tell you how ashamed I am."

"Maddie, please do not beat yourself up about this. He loves you and knows that you love him. That's what matters."

"No Min, I messed up. I appreciate you trying to make

me feel better, but nothing can. I wasn't there."

~~~

I sit by dad's side for two weeks. I hold his hand and watch his forced breathing, I watch the monitors, and I watch time go by as he lies motionless. The doctors want me to say goodbye. They ask me to end it. How can I do this? How can I end his life? What would mom do?

After fourteen days in intensive care, with no sign of recovering—my dad is taken off life support.

It takes him another thirty minutes before he is pronounced dead, as he fights the last few moments, desperate and gurgling for air.

I talk to him, hoping somehow he can hear me, "Dad it's okay, stop fighting. It's time. It's time to go see mom. You believe that? Don't you? That you will see her? She's waiting for you dad. I love you and I am so sorry. Forgive me, forgive me."

Chapter Thirty-Five

He looks peaceful in the coffin that I spent hours picking out, as if it makes a difference what the box that puts him in the ground looks like. As if it will make up for the fact that I left him when he needed me the most. I had him wear his favorite suit, the same one that he wore when he would take mom out on Saturday nights for date night. He always looked so handsome in that suit.

I should be relieved, "He is no longer in pain," everyone says.

"It is for the best."

"He is in a better place."

He is buried alongside mom and I sit by his grave for as long as I can until Min comes to my side and says I have to go.

Back at the house, I fall into his favorite chair in the living room as the crowds of mourners pass by in a gray, black fog, the soft sound of whispered grief fades into the background. I do not know how long I sit for, but it must be for quite a while because I am stiff, and it is dark out when I finally get up and go upstairs to bed.

I have no one left.

No family. I am no longer someone's daughter.

I drift off to an exhausted sleep.

~~~

Min is by my side for the next couple of days. She does not say much but her presence is felt.

I finally get out of bed on the third day after the funeral and muster up the energy to take care of all of the paperwork that goes along with someone dying.

I get a call from dad's attorney, "The house is now yours as well as the money from a modest life insurance policy. I will send you the paperwork that you need to sign to transfer the deed and make a claim with the life insurance."

The life insurance policy will provide me with enough to pay off a few minor debts dad had left. I will use what is remaining of the money to cover the expenses accrued from the funeral as well as cover most of my tuition costs at Walden University.

Not that it really matters.

After spending the next week working out all the details and getting the house set up under my name and dealing with the banks, attorneys, and the funeral home, I finally have a moment to stop and breathe. I use this opportunity to write Jonah who did not attend the funeral, which surprised me. He has called me a couple of times but every time I speak to him, guilt washes over me, tainting the conversation.

Jonah- It has been a difficult couple of weeks for me. It is devastating but I am trying to do the best that I can. He wouldn't want me to dwell on it for too long. What I wouldn't give to hear his voice again, to feel his embrace. I feel so alone in this world. My childhood home is now mine and even though I never planned on creating a life here, I think I will. I love this home and always have. I feel safe here, it feels like home to me. I start school online in August and plan to start looking for a job soon. My lease was up for my apartment and the temporary tenant has moved out. My apartment manager was nice enough to move my stuff to a storage unit for me. I want to go back and move my stuff out of the storage unit soon, and maybe see you, but I am not sure when that will be since I have a lot going on right now. I want you to know that you were never far from my thoughts and that I can't wait to see you. Love –Maddie

I fold the letter and sit back in dad's favorite chair, picking at the peeling green fabric. I check the time and it is already midnight. I head outside so that I can admire the stars while sitting on the front porch swing. The screen door creaks behind me, pinging me with memories of my childhood, worsening the ache for my father.

It takes me a moment before I see the figure walking towards me from the street.

Then it hits me.

Jonah.

It is dark but I can tell he is dressed in jeans and a beat-up looking hoodie. I am faint, as my senses are on overload.

I'm quiet as he walks up to my porch steps and stands in front of me and says, "I thought you might need some company."

Unable to speak, I turn around and open the front door, motioning him inside. We have spent many months using words but right now, I have no words left. All I want to do is hold him. He comes inside and I follow, the screen creaking behind me. I turn the deadbolt and collapse on the floor in a flood of tears. I have cried so much since dad died; I did not think I had any tears left. I do not have the energy to be embarrassed in front of Jonah although I am sure this is not the welcome he envisioned.

Jonah sits on the floor by my side and wraps me in a bear hug as I weep into his hoodie. He never says a word; he just holds me as I cry. I fall asleep like this, on the floor in his arms.

Chapter Thirty-Six

I wake up and lift my head to look up at Jonah. He is asleep, leaned back against the wall. He looks so lovely; his mouth is open slightly, and the moonlight from the nearby window casts a soft gleam across his features. I gently trace the light running across his jawline with my thumb and he opens his eyes. He leans down and kisses me. It is a sweet kiss but salty from the tears that have dried on my face and lips.

I stand up and extend my hand.

We walk up the stairs slowly, hand in hand, and when we get to my bedroom, I flip on a lamp by the bed. Jonah does not immediately follow me in but stays in the doorway. It is a bit too warm in the room, so I walk to the large windows and open them slightly, allowing the night air to breeze in, the moonlight dancing across the floor and onto the bed. The air is crisp; a few snowflakes drift in with the breeze, reminding me that wintertime isn't so bad.

Jonah's hands are in his pockets and he looks unsettled as I wordlessly begin to undress.

I take my time.

He watches me with big eyes that are darkened by the shadows in the room. He appears to catch his breath as I get down to just my bra and underwear. He carefully strolls over; peering down at me as he gently touches my face.

Before I know it, his mouth is on mine. His lips are soft but eager.

He tastes good.

I feel limp as he lifts me off my feet and lays me down on the bed. I watch him intently as he takes off his hoodie and then slides off his black t-shirt over his shoulders, exposing his chest.

Such a simple thing, a chest.

There is something deeply intimate about seeing a man shirtless for the first time; a man you desire to see all of, exposing his body to you. His chest is strong with just a sprinkling of hair.

I drink him in; I savor the moment in its perfection. He stares at me darkly as he unzips and lets his jeans drop to the floor. He climbs on top of me, putting one hand on each side of my head as he looms over me in all his beauty. His face reads as though he is in disbelief, as though he never really thought that this moment would happen.

With that look, I can no longer contain myself. I kiss him hard and run my hands all over his body. He groans deeply as I gently nip at his bottom lip. We tear off what few items of clothing we have left and in one quick move; he puts on a condom and is inside of me.

The shock of penetration combined with the intense pleasure that comes with it causes me to arch my back and moan. Jonah clenches his jaw and bites his lip as he slides in and out of me, leading me to orgasm quickly.

Jonah whispers in my ear as I writhe in ecstasy beneath him, "I love you, Maddie." I barely manage to respond, "I. Love. You. Too."

We drift into a long night of passion, and I lose myself completely, thinking of nothing but love and pleasure, hoping this will erase the pain.

Chapter Thirty-Seven

The sun is streaming in through the open windows. A slight breeze is in the air, so I snuggle closer to Jonah, the warmth from the blankets surrounding me. Happiness glides over every inch of my body and I smile. I turn my head to see him sleeping soundly. In the morning sunlight, he is sublime. Watching him sleep, my happiness begins to wane as "hurry Maddie" flashes in my mind's eye, haunting me.

"Good morning," I say trying to sound normal.

"Mornin'," he says quietly, rubbing his eyes.

"How'd you get here last night?" I inquire.

"I took a bus and then it was just a short walk here. It was late so I wasn't sure if you'd be sleeping, so when you walked out, I was still trying to figure out if I should knock or go get a hotel room instead."

Impressed I say, "Well I'm really glad you are here."

"Me too. I couldn't think of anywhere else I would rather be."

I blush and try to gather myself, "I wanted to tell you that I have a check for the profit from your story we published. It's not a lot of money, but it is a couple of hundred dollars. That should tide you over for a little while."

"Really? I've made money from my story?"

"Yeah, pretty great, huh?"

"Hell yeah."

We both laugh. It feels good to laugh. I have not laughed in a long time. I have never seen Jonah laugh before; it is slightly odd and unexpected which makes me laugh even harder; breaking up some of the awkwardness we are experiencing.

Something is off though, and I cannot shake the feeling that the bliss of this moment is fleeting.

Jonah's face changes slightly; a clenched jaw and furrowed brow indicate tension. A sense of dread washes over me.

"Is something wrong?" My hand is on his chest; his heart is beating too fast.

"I need to tell you something, Maddie."

Oh no.

"What? What is it, Jonah?"

"I don't want to hurt you, but I did want to let you know that I have been seeing someone."

"What? Who? How? You were just released not even

a month ago." I am sitting up now.

"Okay here goes . . . an old girlfriend of mine reached out to me after she saw an article online. I haven't talked to her since my arrest. We were never very serious but when she saw that I was released, she wanted to contact me and tell me that she had a child. She said I'm the father. I wanted to be sure, so I had a paternity test done. I've been kind of getting reacquainted with her and trying to get to know the child. I'm sorry I didn't say anything to you."

"Why didn't you? Last night would never have happened if I had known about this!"

"I know. That's probably why I didn't say anything. I wanted to be with you even if it was brief."

"You ASSHOLE. How selfish are you?" Not as selfish as me, my inner voice screams.

"Very. I'm sorry Maddie. Please don't hate me over this."

We are both standing in the bedroom now; his hands raised protectively, as though I am going to attack him. What does he think of me? Then it hits me, he does not know me at all.

"Jonah, I'm not going to attack you, you can relax.

The truth is you do not know me at all and that's clear to me now. I don't know what I was thinking. This was all a mistake. Why did you say that you loved me?"

"Because I do. I do love you Maddie. I'm just trying to do the right thing, for once, I want to do the right thing. I just want to try to make this work with Emily and my son, I have a chance at a real family, and I don't want to mess it up." I am fighting back tears.

"Please, can't we at least be friends? Keep writing to each other? I don't want to lose you."

"I don't think so, Jonah. I don't think that would be a good idea. I feel completely betrayed. Please get out." Please get out before I cry.

"I'm so sorry Maddie. I will leave. Please just think about this though. Call me, write me. I want you in my life."

"Please Jonah, just leave. I don't want to talk to you about this anymore."

And just like that, he is gone.

Chapter Thirty-Eight

My heart sinks to the soles of my feet, weighing them down as I walk across the floor. My insecurities rise along with my anger. How could he do this? He told me he loved me. Did he mean it? Was I just for sex? Am I the biggest fool in the world? Borderline frantic, I call Min. I need advice, fast.

"Min, Jonah was here and spent the night with me but then I told him to leave because he said he has a kid with someone he used to know and…"

"Whoa, whoa, whoa, Maddie. Slow down. So, he stayed the night with you, and then he told you he has a kid?"

"Yes, some woman he was with before he was sentenced had a kid. He says he hasn't spoken to the woman at all until she saw an article online about him and how he was released, and she contacted him."

"Is he sure the child is his?"

"Yes, he took a paternity test."

"Oh, man. So now what? Does he still want to be with you? Do you still want to be with him?"

"He said this is his chance at a real family and he

doesn't want to screw it up. He is trying to work things out with her. Her name is Emily." I officially hate that name now.

"Wow. I'm shocked Maddie. I don't know what to say." I am crying again, apparently, this is my new thing.

"I can't believe it. I can't believe I fell for him. What was I thinking? I don't even know him," I say, sniffling.

"Love is a funny thing Maddie, it blinds you, it makes you do things you never thought possible. Please don't be this upset."

"I'm so lost and completely foolish. I lost everything, my job, the respect of my peers, my dad, and for what? Absolutely nothing."

"But maybe you have gained something else, Maddie."

"Like what?"

"A new perspective? A fresh start? Change? You said yourself that you are unhappy. Maybe the universe is trying to rattle you so that you can learn something."

"I don't know what it is trying to teach me Min, but I don't want to feel this way anymore."

"I know you don't, but embrace it, Maddie. Learn from it. I promise you; you will come out of this a better version of yourself."

"He said he loved me Min. Was it all a lie? What if it was all just to get me into bed?"

"Maddie, you tell me. Is that really what you believe?"

The truth is that no I do not believe he just used me. I know by his letters and by the way he held me that he does care about me.

"Min, I know you're right. I am just all over the place. I just didn't want to lose him."

"You don't have to. Write to him. You need to focus on your own journey now Maddie, not jumping into a relationship. You lost your father, your job, hell you were shot Maddie; there's no way you could have a relationship right now, at least not a healthy one. This is for the best. You have to realize that. I mean, where did you believe this would go? Did you really think you were going to have a serious relationship with a convict who just got out of prison? Be honest with yourself."

I know she is right, what was I planning on doing? Marrying Jonah?

After I hang up and calm down, I write him a letter.

Jonah- My first instinct while writing this letter is to

tell you that I am angry and hurt. But the truth is that this is for the best. With me just losing my dad and going through so many changes in my life, I am not in a place to have a full-on relationship with anyone, even you. When you were here, I knew something was off. Something did not seem quite right, and I kept wondering how we were ever going to make this work. I have repeatedly been selfish since the day I met you, putting my own desires before my job, even the needs of my dear father. My desire to fulfill my fantasy with you has severely cost me. It is something that I need to reflect on. This is not your fault, it is mine. I have some serious soul searching to do. Congratulations on learning that you are a father. Also, thank you. Thank you for saving my life. I will never regret loving you or the time we spent together. Write to me sometime, if you wish- Maddie.

Chapter Thirty-Nine

The next few weeks are the hardest. I miss my dad and, as usual, I miss my mother. Loneliness, my old friend, keeps me company as I meander around in this big house alone.

On Sunday morning, as I sit drinking coffee in dad's favorite chair, I think about what dad and I shared in his last few months. His words about my mom circle in my head, and his wishes for me to travel like mom always wanted to keep coming to me, reminding me of the box of mom's he told me about.

"Where is that?" I say aloud to the ghosts around me.

I search all over the house, regretting not asking him for it before he became too ill. Opening the closet in the bedroom that mom and dad shared, for the first time since dad died, I switch the light on and pull down linens from the top shelf. Behind the linens are several shoeboxes and one plain brown box that looks a bit different. I pull the box down; a layer of dust coats the top along with a couple of dead flies.

With the box placed on the bed, it seems ordinary. A simple, plain, brown box with nothing written on it.

However, on the inside, it is anything but.

An extensive collection of travel guides and images cut from magazines; images from all over the world. I am rummaging through The Great Wall of China and the green fields of Ireland when I notice a small brown leather journal stuck to the right side.

I run my finger over the brown material, taking in the smell of ink and old leather. The pages are filled with handwritten quotes regarding all aspects of life, but the majority are about traveling.

Quotes such as "Travelling- it leaves you speechless, then turns you into a storyteller- Ibn Battuta,"

"The mountains are calling, and I must go- Muir,"

And "You don't always need a plan. Sometimes you just need to breathe, trust, let go and see what happens- Mandy Hale."

The collection is both beautiful and melancholy.

To know that my mother had such a desire to travel, but never did, pains me. I never saw this side of my mother. I never knew her to be anything but happy. I wish I had known her as a real person, instead of this image I have built in my mind of a happy, prepared for anything, perfect mother. I did not get the chance to know her as an adult, as friends.

The first page of the journal has the quote by Atticus that dad reminded me of, written in my mother's handwriting: "Never go in search of love, go in search of life, and life will find you the love you seek."

As I contemplate the meaning behind the quote, I notice that the largest portion of the images and guides in her treasure chest are of Paris. It appears that my mother wanted to go to Paris more than anywhere else in the world.

Inspiration slaps me across the face.

I will go to Paris and follow the steps she regretted not taking, in search of life.

I grab my phone, make yet another, previously believed out-of-character, choice, and purchase a plane ticket.

Who am I?

The question enters my mind and I respond aloud, "I am still trying to figure that out."

Chapter Forty

I land in Paris on a Thursday afternoon and as I walk out of the airport and look around, it dawns on me that I know absolutely nothing about the city, other than the stereotypical notions of snobby French people and croissants. I also do not know a lick of French. I hail a cab and give the driver the address of the apartment that I booked. Luckily, he understands a bit of English. While we drive, I keep my eyes wide open to the views around me.

Wow.

The city is old and gray with a slight drizzly rain flowing down the marble statues, that seem to be on every corner. It is exquisite. I suddenly wish I had an expensive camera to attempt to capture this beauty.

The driver drops me off at a gray stone building with red doors. I pay him with the Euros I exchanged my dollars for at the airport and walk briskly with my luggage over to the red door with the numbers **562** printed in black letters on a small metal tag. To the right side of the door, there is a lockbox, I use a combination code to open it and get the key. With some force, the red door pushes open to a small entryway that is sparse but for a red umbrella leaning against the wall to the left.

I drop my bags down, walk into a room painted in red and tan, accessorized with matching furniture and modern abstract art. Most of the space is wide-open except for a separate room with a small bed and an even smaller bathroom. The kitchen is off to the right-hand side of the living area with a counter and two high bar stools. While tiny, the apartment is well kept and in an incredibly central location (according to what I read) and I am struck by how lucky I am to have gotten this spot without any research.

Maybe it is not always necessary to plan for everything.

It is early afternoon when I arrive so I unpack and try to get some sleep so I can go exploring later in the evening. I hit the mattress hard and pass out from jet lag.

A solid five hours of sleep later, I wake discombobulated.

It is now after six p.m. and the drizzle outside has stopped but now a wash of what I have done envelops me.

"What the hell am I doing here?"

I remember Dr. Abby telling me to try it, that she thought being spontaneous might be good for me and I hope she, my father, and Min are right. I step in the shower that is just big enough for me to stand and instantly realize that I forgot to pack shampoo and conditioner and the room does not have any available.

"Some things are good to prepare for," I say aloud, chastising myself. It dawns on me that I forgot to pack my day planner so I cannot even write a note to remind myself to pick up shampoo.

How fitting.

Taking it as a sign, I shrug and think that maybe I do not need my planner after all. I rinse off, wrap a white towel around my body, head back to the bedroom and sit on the bed. So unsure about what to do with myself, I look up travel tips on my phone and pull out the travel guide mother had. I also download a translation app on my phone so I can communicate in French as needed. I finally get up the courage to get dressed and leave the apartment to start exploring.

Pulling open the red door, I glimpse to my left and my right and take out my phone to view a map.

Suddenly emboldened by the bustling of the city

around me, and wishing to make the most of this whim, I put my phone back in my bag before I have a chance to look at it and go with my gut instead.

"Left sounds good."

Apparently in addition to crying, talking to myself is now another thing I do all the time.

The words in mother's journal ring in my ear, "You don't always need a plan. Sometimes you just need to breathe, trust, let go and see what happens," and while she never lived her own life by these words, I wonder if she is trying to tell me something now, teach me something that she wished someone had taught her.

Her presence is felt as I trek along on this confusing journey.

Chapter Forty-One

Have you ever stared at yourself in the mirror and had no idea who you were? Have you ever felt so lost that you do something completely out of character? Have you ever thought that everything you ever knew about yourself was wrong? Have you ever been faced with an ugly truth about yourself and want nothing more than to change? Well, that is how I felt when I first arrived in Paris. I have heard about people going through midlife crises where they cheat on their spouses, get makeovers, and buy fancy cars. I am aware of what psychologists and philosophers alike call an "existential crisis" in which people look back at their lives and wonder if it meant anything or if their entire existence has been pointless. Even though I am educated in these phenomena, I never imagined they would happen to me. Not Madeline, class president. Not Madeline, the one with the perfect grades. Not Madeline, the one with her whole life planned. I believed I was too rational of a person to have any kind of life crisis.

Yet. Here I am.

Everything in my life changed, from my marriage to

my career, to what I thought I knew about love, to what I want to do with my life, to the very core of who I am. Now I find myself in the throes of a full-on classic crisis. This is a crisis of character. I do not know who I am or what I believe anymore.

So, what do I do?

Instead of buying a fancy car or getting a makeover, I fly to Paris, a city I have never been to before with no plan. I have no idea what the hell I am going to do here.

~~~

What can I even say about Paris that has already been said? Let me try.

The first four days in Paris, I spend shedding my anxiety. I walk everywhere. I go to the museums, the Eiffel Tower, the Louvre and many cafés and bookshops. I spend my time walking all over the city and try to take it all in, the sights, the smells, the food, trying to exist in the moment.

Instead of burying myself in worry and getting lost in my anxious thoughts, I consume myself with Paris, and bit by bit, my anxiety decreases; my happiness begins to flow to the top. As I explore, I only speak when I have to and, instead, spend my time listening. I listen to the accents, the words, the many various sounds of the city from the traffic to the low hum of people bustling about. While immersing myself in Parisian culture, it does not take me long to fall in love. Not with a person, but with a place.

Paris.

Now I understand why my mother always wanted to visit this place. Like a great novel, the city's mysteries begin to reveal themselves to me as the days turn like pages. The city flutters with life during the day creating an intoxicating world that I am thrilled to be a part of. Each moment, the city explodes with light, color, movement, and sound, compelling me to take part in the excitement of life versus just watching it.

It is now day seven and I desire to start speaking to humans again. The couple that lives in the same apartment building as me, are young and they speak English occasionally. It is just about noon and I wait to hear them opening their door, as they usually leave their apartment about this time every day. It is a bit silly, but I want to "bump" into them and casually make conversation.

I can hear footsteps and low voices, so I quickly grab

my bag and open my door, hoping to catch them before leaving.

Yes. They are right beside me pulling the door shut behind them as I open mine.

"Bonjour," I say with a kind smile.

Please be my friend.

"Bonjour, ça va?"

"I am well thank you. Sorry, I don't know much more French. I am learning though. Do you speak English?"

"Oui, yes, we speak English too. We are Norwegian. Are you American?"

"Yes, I am actually. Norway? That is amazing, why are you here in Paris?"

"We are here staying for a year. I'm a painter, my husband is a musician. I have my art display here that the school I attend back home is hosting. What about you? You here for work?"

"Well actually no. I am just visiting for a month. I have never been and just decided to visit."

"How adventurous of you, are you alone?"

"Yeah, it's just me. I've been here for a week now."

"Wonderful, we've been here for about six months already."

They exchange words in their native tongue before turning back to me, "My name is Kim, and this is Alex. Would you like to join us for lunch? We have a great spot."

"Would it be too much of an imposition?"

"No! Please, join us!"

Kim and Alex are genuine, big smiles grace their faces with ease. They are kind enough to take me to some of the best spots in Paris over the next couple of weeks, always stopping by my door and asking me to join them. To meet such kind people is refreshing, encouraging me to be more like them.

Thanks to their insight, I can indulge in the best food I have ever had and at night, I explore my newfound love: dancing.

I was never one to go to nightclubs when I was in my twenties. I was always too serious for those kinds of activities. I never danced before; even at my wedding, I was too embarrassed to dance in front of people, too concerned about what others thought of me. I took life so seriously; I am annoyed with myself for missing these magical moments.

The first time we go to a club, Kim shares with me

some of her wisdom, "You are so tense, Miss Maddie. Why? Are you not happy right now?"

"Oh yes, I am. I am just somewhat nervous. I don't know how to dance."

"No, you don't need to know how to dance, to dance. It's something more. What's bothering you?"

"I was just thinking about my parents. My dad died recently, and I am just missing him. I was not there for him at the end when he needed me, and I feel so guilty about it."

"Ohhh I see Miss Maddie. Dancing will help."

"Huh? How so?"

"Simple. Letting go and forgiving yourself. Dancing helps with that."

As I sway under the red lights of the Moulin Rouge, Kim's words compel me to embrace the art of letting go. Therefore, I let go. I let go of the pain of losing my parents, let go of the guilt, let go of getting fired, let go of Jonah, let go of fear, let go of trying to control everything, and in turn, depression begins to let go of me. Dancing is not a cure-all, it may only provide a brief intermission to my ongoing journey to find happiness, but as I twirl under the glitter that rains down from above, glistening against the red lights, reflecting the sparkling of my soul, I am free.

Chapter Forty-Two

Once I started letting go of my need to control, my insecurities, my anxieties, my shame, something happened, something unexpected. Happiness. This unexpected change occurred when I was not paying attention; it seeped into my consciousness one glorious morning when I was enjoying a croissant and a warm cup of tea, watching the flow of people pass by as I sat at a table outside of my, newly discovered, and favorite café.

The croissant falls apart in my mouth, practically melting with buttery goodness and I smile. It then occurs to me that I have been doing that a lot lately, smiling. I smile as I people watch, smile as I eat delicious food, smile as I dance, smile as I talk to new friends.

Happiness is the only explanation.

How have I gone my whole life without feeling the way I do right now? Do not get me wrong, there were moments, fleeting glimpses of happiness during my childhood. Sitting with mom and dad on the beach watching the sun go down, snuggled together at the ice cream shop with my mother; enjoying our Friday treats or laughing with Min during one of our many conversations, stealing a kiss, receiving a letter from someone I loved, reconnecting with my father.

Happiness I believed to be fleeting and rare, like the light from a firefly, only illuminating in short spurts throughout its brief life.

Sitting here in the morning light of Paris, soaking in the glow radiating from the sun, it dawns on me that happiness should not be transient. Instead, it should be felt often; embraced to its fullest and held on to for as long as possible because, one day, just like the light from the firefly, it will go dark and this journey will come to an end.

This is what it is all about; finding happiness and it does not come from some plan, some naïve attempt at control, but from within. The joy I am feeling is coming from me, not my job, not a husband, not Jonah, not from any external sources.

Just me.

I cannot believe it never occurred to me before.

~~~

It's a slightly gloomy afternoon as I make my way down to the famed bookstore, *Shakespeare and Company*. The city is subdued thanks to the cloudy skies that are producing a hazy cast covering the landscape around me. Most of its residents are busy at work while I enjoy the calmness that only a gray Tuesday afternoon can bring.

I pick a corner nook to read Jane Austin. I'm enjoying every delicate word that she so intricately wrote when I look up at the clock on the wall, only to see that I have been sitting in this spot for three hours. It is amazing how a good book can weave time in such an unrecognizable way.

I use this break from Austin to take in the sights around me. The small spaces between shelves, books crammed into every crevice and cranny; creaky stairs that are so narrow, the people walking up have to wait for the others coming down; the low hum of conversation, whispers about the beauty of the store; the store cat, sitting on a cushion, unabashed. I breathe in a long breath, filling my lungs with the smell of vanilla coming from the old books so that I may remember this moment, and this place, forever.

With one last glance around before I head back to my apartment, I stand up to leave but something catches my eye. Well, *someone* catches my eye. A man is leaned against a corner bookcase, looking at a book with such intensity; I feel as though I am witnessing something that I should not, something private. Before I can look away, he must feel my gaze because he sees me, and we lock eyes. I should be embarrassed, but he smiles at me and it is lovely; set against a backdrop of dark, wavy hair. With a dusting of black facial hair further accentuating his blue eyes, I think "wow." His lean long hands close the book slowly as I hope he comes over to speak to me.

~~~

His name is Ellis and he is an avid collector of rare books, I learn during our conversation over coffee.

"I have an amazing collection, books from all over the world, some written in languages I don't understand but bound so beautifully I had to buy them," he says enthusiastically.

"How wonderful," I say displaying my envy, "the passion you feel for books is sensational. I can tell you are American from your accent, but do you live in Paris?"

"I'm only here on business; I live in New York."

"What's your business?" I ask, trying in vain not to stare at his lips.

"I own a marketing company that provides social

medical consulting to companies all over the world. I won't lie, it is a great life. I get to do the things I love the most, traveling and finding old books. What about you?"

"Well, I came here on a whim. I've never traveled outside of the U.S. before. I was working for the F.B.I. but lost my job and have spent many months being a full-time caretaker for my dad before he passed."

"Oh, I'm so sorry to hear about your dad. I lost my mother last year to cancer. I miss her so much."

"I lost my mother to cancer years ago and I'm still not over it."

We spend the afternoon walking along the banks of the Seine, talking about everything from our parents, to my job at the F.B.I., my crazy last twelve months, how I ended up here in Paris, to the entanglement with a convict that started it all. I even tell him about my deep shame of me not being with my father when he needed me the most. I figure I need to be honest about who I am, not only for Ellis's sake but for my own. I have no desire to be anything but honest anymore; he shares his secrets with me and me with him.

There is something about Ellis putting me at ease, a sense of simplicity that I have never felt before. All I want to do is be near him.

That night, still unwilling to part ways, Ellis offers to cook dinner for me at my apartment but before he starts cooking, we sit on my couch to enjoy a glass of wine while every inch of my body wills him to kiss me.

"Thanks for offering to cook dinner Ellis. I have to say, I didn't expect to end tonight like this."

"Me neither," he says laughing, "but I'm so glad I did."

Not wanting my nervous energy to be obvious, I take a big sip of Merlot, allowing the soft finish to coat my mouth and throat in confidence.

Ellis looks at me as though he has just discovered the rarest book of them all and reaches over, puts his hand on the back of my head, bringing my lips up to his, ending my torture. We never make it to dinner as we fall into each other, making love all night long.

~~~

During my last next week in Paris, Ellis and I spend as much time together as possible, only briefly parting when he has to attend a meeting for work. I start to expect he intentionally extended his stay in the City of Love thanks to a few conversations I overheard him have on the phone.

Ellis leaves Paris to embark on a lengthy international tour as I leave to head back home. Neither of us thinks it realistic to try to have a relationship spanning such great distances and I know that I should stay single for a while. I want to keep focusing on myself before I try to commit to anyone.

Therefore, we part ways.

Saying goodbye to Ellis was difficult but I knew that someday, somehow, we would see each other again. I could tell it was just the beginning of our story.

With my trip over, I am heartbroken to leave Paris. I have learned to love the city and it has begun to feel like home. I have an adequate French vocabulary and a deep admiration of French food and culture. I have also made lifelong friends with Alexander and Kim and I promise to visit them in Norway. I came to Paris overwhelmed, lost, confused, and looking for a way to connect with my parents, and in the throes of a transformation that began over a year prior. I am leaving Paris with a deeper understanding of not only who I am, but also who I aspire to be.

I am a cliché because I leave knowing that Paris will

never leave me, understanding that the cliché exists for a reason.

Chapter Forty-Three

I am back in the States and relieved to find my home is still in order, suffering no damage or break-ins while I was away. Min emailed and texted me several times during my trip and the tone of them is of worry, so I give her a call first.

"Hey Min, I'm back, how are you?"

"Maddie! Oh my gosh, I haven't heard your voice in so long! It's so good to hear from you. How the hell was it? Did you have a blast?"

"It was amazing Min, I loved it. It was genuinely the best experience of my life. We have to get together soon so I can tell you everything. How are you though? How is your family? Anything new with you?"

Min sounds good as she responds, "Things have been good. The family is great. They are as wonderful as ever. The job is good. Our car broke down and my mother had a health scare but she's okay now. I've been doing well and have not had a single drink for over a month now. It was hard at first but I'm starting to feel a lot better. Man, I've sure missed talking to you."

"Me too Min, I'm so happy to hear that you have been

doing well. We need to get together soon so we can catch up."

"Yes, we do! I'll call you later and let you know after I talk with Raymond when I will be able to get up there to visit, maybe this weekend. I'll let you go and get settled."

"That'd be great, talk to you soon."

After we get off the phone, I make a quick run to pick up all of my mail. As I walk out of the post office, I flip through many envelopes and spot a letter from Jonah.

Jonah.

I smile as I think of him. I open the letter quickly and read:

Maddie- I tried calling you but could not get through and was worried you changed your phone number on me so I thought I would send you a letter. I want you to know that I have been thinking about you a lot and just want to say that I am so sorry I did not tell you everything that was going on with me. I care about you so much and the last thing that I want is for you to feel used.

I have not been doing so well. I miss you and think of you all the time. I know I said I wanted to try to make things work with Emily, but I just find myself wishing I was with you. Can we try again? Can you give me another chance? I am starting to be acquainted with my son and Emily and I are a bit rocky but we are trying to figure out how to make this co-parenting thing work. I want to be on good terms with her so that she will let me keep seeing him.

Thank you for everything you have given me and done for me. If you do not want to call, please write and let me know if I can have another chance. Love – Jonah

The letter is unexpected. It fills me up with warmth, but I do not have the same reaction to a letter from Jonah as I used to. Something has changed, and I realize it is me. I think the best thing to do would be to call him and explain. As the phone rings, it suddenly dawns on me that I do not even know what I am going to say if he answers.

"Maddie?"

All I can muster is a pathetic, "Hey."

"Hey, how are you? I haven't heard from you in a while. I tried calling you. Is everything okay?"

"Yes, everything is great actually. I went on a trip alone spontaneously. I've been in Paris for the last month and just got back yesterday."

"Paris?" He sounds stunned, "Maddie that is amazing! Was it awesome?"

"Yes, it was Jonah and I want to tell you all about it. Listen, I just got your letter. How have you been this month?"

He responds slowly, "I've been okay. Just piecing my life together, trying to hold down my job, taking classes to get my GED, and trying to get to know my kid but that has been harder than I thought . . . I've missed you."

"Thank you for that Jonah. I wanted to call and tell you that I think we should just be friends. Something was not right when we were together that night and even though it was wonderful and I will never forget it, I'm not looking to be in a relationship right now. Plus, you have a chance at something great, a family, and I encourage you to keep working on that. I'm going to focus on getting back into school and finding a job I enjoy and hopefully finding time to travel more."

The words come out a little too quickly as I hope I am not hurting him, "I want to stay in touch, and I want to keep you in my life but let's stick to friendship and letters if that is okay with you." I wait for his response.

His breath catches and he says, "Okay Maddie, I will

take what I can get. I'm happy to be friends."

Chapter Forty-Four

One Year and Sometime Later . . .

The holiday season is in full swing. On my way to attend a Christmas party at Min's, I stop at the mall in a hurry, desperate to find Lizzy the perfect gift. My heels are pinching my toes as I clack along like a lost reindeer. She is the only child I buy for each year, so I take this task very seriously. Luckily, Min is always helpful and provides me with some hints as to what Lizzy would like. The latest Justin Bieber themed hoodie is on the hot list this year. Min gets the same thing she always does, a renewed subscription to a wine of the month club, and Raymond a box of cigars.

As I clank past a window with Italian wines on display, I stop in my tracks. One wine specifically catches my eye: Sangiovese.

This particular wine reminds me of a recent trip taken to Italy. It was Kim and Alex's idea and they brought along a few of their friends and I brought along a few of mine including Min and Ellis. I paid for Min's plane ticket as a gift to celebrate her year and a half of sobriety, and to thank her for always being by my side, Raymond fully approved and flew out to join her so they could spend quality time together.

Ellis and I had started following each other on social media after Paris and even though we had not communicated directly with each other, when I sent him a message asking if he would like to join us in Italy, he responded simply with "Yes."

Ellis met us in a small villa, a couple of days after we had arrived. We were all sitting at a large table at an outdoor café based at the foot of a hillside, drinking Sangiovese and soaking in the Tuscan sun when Ellis came strolling up the old road towards me. His lean body and broad grin immediately took me back to our rendezvous in Paris in the best way possible.

My nerves were shot as I waited for his arrival, stressed that this may have been a mistake as we only spent a brief time together and maybe he was not as marvelous as I remembered. Once I laid eyes on him, however, those nerves melted away and flowed from me onto the cobblestones beneath my feet as I raced over and jumped into his arms.

We spent the next four days roaming from villa to villa, living each moment as though they were fading stars, clinging to them tightly before they dimmed into eternity.

As I stare at the bottle in the window display, I can still feel the warmth of the Italian sun on my skin and the coolness of the wine against the back of my throat, and I smile. I smile such a smile that my happiness must be contagious as an old woman walking by smiles too.

"You must love that wine as much as I do the way you are smiling at it," she says, voice raspy.

"Can you wait here one second?"

"Sure, dear."

I come out of the shop a couple of moments later and hand her a bottle, "Merry Christmas ma'am."

"Oh, thank you so much, dear. Merry Christmas to you too."

The little lady walks away, smiling and holding her gift, and I am left fulfilled. Life is good.

Chapter Forty-Five

Two More Years Later

The air is frigid as I walk briskly to my car after leaving the Police Department. With three months from graduating with my Ph.D. in Forensic Psychology from Walden University, I have not had a moment to slow down. Working full time as the resident behavior analyst with the Frederick Police Department has filled my days with copious amounts of coffee and anxiety followed by evenings full of more coffee and anxiety-ridden schoolwork. With all of the coffee and anxiety, it might be surprising to know that I am happy.

Traveling has become my passion. Traveling with little planning is completely out of character for who I used to be. Now, it is my favorite thing about myself. I can be spontaneous and adventurous but just never loosened up enough to realize it before; I was consumed with controlling every moment and following some life plan that I had created for myself as a child. To capitalize on my newly found spontaneous side, I never plan my trips more than two weeks in advance. These adventures of mine have been the very definition of self-care; forcing me to look at myself and grow, change, and shed all of my preconceived notions about myself, human nature, and life itself.

When I look back over the last few years of my life, I am proud of myself. I went from someone whose entire world fell apart and was completely lost and miserable, to confident and happy. I have faced the harsh reality of my selfishness and learned to be a better person.

Over the past few years, I have not seen Jonah. However, we still do write to each other. He has written me a dozen or so times a year and I to him. Mainly we write about what is going on in our lives and the progress we are both making. I talk about work, school, and my travels; he talks about trying to rebuild his life. He has maintained a relationship with his Aunt Lisa and his cousins, completed his GED, and has an excellent relationship with his son.

We talk about many things, but we never talk about us. I do not know if he is dating anyone and he never asks me about my love life. Our relationship is one of friendship and I value it immensely. He was able to publish a book of short stories and completed an autobiography, which he mailed to me. He titled it *The*

Beautiful Bandit: My Journey to Freedom. In it is an entire chapter about me titled *Sarah*. It is amazing to hear him describe our relationship through his eyes.

My favorite part reads, "Her light was so powerful; it cut through the thick darkness encasing my life. She will never truly know the impact she has had on me. She brought me from the brink of ending it all. She says I saved her, but really, she saved me."

To make things better, the book is doing very well and has popped up on several 'best reads' lists.

It is now a bright day in May as I check my mailbox and admire the new flower buds on the trees lining the street. I smile at the letter from Jonah congratulating me on finishing school. Today is finally commencement and I have a flight to Tampa, Florida, where the home base for Walden University is. I am so happy to have Min and her family making the trip with me to show their love and support since I cannot have either of my parents there. As I walk back into the house to grab my suitcase and head to the airport, I notice flowers sitting on my porch. They are congratulations from Dr. Flanigan, Tammy, and Henry. Dave and I are no longer in contact and about six months ago, Tammy called me to tell me that Dave had been fired for misconduct. She does not share the details just that karma had found him. I just think to myself about how karma came for me and I find myself emphatic for Dave. After all, I know better than anyone how selfish decisions can cost you everything.

Tammy and I talk often and meet up for lunch on occasion. She has turned out to be a great friend and I'm embarrassed to say, it took me too long to notice it. I spend time making it up to her now.

A colorful bouquet sitting to the right of the white porch swing has a card reading, "Congrats dear friend cannot wait to see you in Ireland in September! - Love Kim and Alex." To my surprise, I do not see anything from Ellis, but I am sure he will call me later. He always does so I am not going to dwell. I am not going to let anything stop me from enjoying this day.

At commencement, I practically float across the stage to receive my diploma. I am genuinely proud of myself. Afterward, I go out to dinner with Min and her family. Her daughter Lizzy is now a fully-fledged teenager and it is funny to see Min and Raymond try to navigate these challenges. Min and I head out for drinks after dinner so that we can celebrate and catch up since we have not seen each other much lately.

As we sip on a couple of martinis at a colorful bar with blue lights, Min says, "I'm so proud of you Maddie, how are feeling about finally being done with your degree?"

I smile big as I say, "I'm thrilled. I'm ready to be done with school. I want to start teaching courses on Forensics in the evenings after work."

"That sounds great Maddie. What about a personal life though? Have you put much thought into starting to date again?"

I sigh, "I don't know. I haven't put much thought into it because I have been so busy."

Min nods and says, "I see, I hope you don't get offended Maddie, but I want to be frank and say something to you and I hope you don't mind. You're brilliant and successful Maddie, but I don't want you to miss out on love. It's the best thing."

"I know Min; I don't want to miss out on it either. I want to be in a relationship someday but I'm not going to seek it. It will find me when it is right.

Min rolls her eyes and says, "If you change your mind, I have a few eligible bachelors I could set you up with."

I laugh aloud at this, "Of course you do Min, but for now, can we celebrate my accomplishment and enjoy each other?"

With that Min smiles, "Absolutely girl. Let's drink to that."

~~~

The next morning, I take a flight out of Tampa back to D.C. and make the drive back home to Frederick.

I pull into my driveway, but I do not immediately notice a person sitting on the front porch. I shut the car door and walk up the steps oblivious. It is not until he calls my name that I look up in surprise to see Ellis.

Fudge-sticks.

He is more handsome than ever, his bright blue eyes shimmering as he smiles.

As he walks down the steps of my childhood home, enmeshed in the early afternoon sun, time slows to the brink of stopping completely.

From some distant place, I hear a faint, "Hey."

The only response I can muster is an underwhelming, "Hello."

He continues with, "I'm sorry to surprise you. I thought about calling but I thought it would be best if I just showed up."

Ellis pulls a single red rose from his back pocket and hands it to me, the petals slightly askew thanks to being carried in his back pocket, yet, somehow, I still think it might be the most beautiful flower I have ever seen.

"Congrats on the degree Maddie. I'm so impressed, you are really something," he motions behind him to the two dozen roses sitting on the porch. "I didn't think one bouquet was enough."

I take the rose and clutch it to my chest, gathering all of the strength I can to respond. "Thank you, Ellis. What are you doing here?"

"I was in Baltimore for work and remembered that you said you lived in Frederick. I'm not going to lie I contacted your friend Min and got your address. I hope that is okay, I wanted to surprise you to tell you congratulations in person."

"Of course, it's okay, I'm thrilled you are here. Min didn't say anything to me." No wonder she lectured me on the importance of love!

"Maddie, I'm not here looking for a brief encounter like the ones we have had before, I wanted to ask you if we could be together, you know do this thing for real."

I am so shocked I cannot speak. I open my mouth, but no words come out.

He continues, "I think you're amazing and I've never been happier than the moments I spend with you. You're such a beacon of joy that all I want to do is be in your presence. It seems like a waste not to give this a real chance. What do you think?"

No words are necessary as I stand on my tiptoes to reach up for a kiss.

Chapter Forty-Six

The last chapter of this book –
but the beginning of the rest of Maddie's life.

The salty wind whips through my hair, reminding me of the cable knitted hat I bought at the beginning of our trip to the Emerald Isle. I pull the hat out of my coat pocket, unwrapping its thick fabric, and quickly tug it on. Relief comes as my ears begin to tingle with warmth.

It is a cool September evening with the Atlantic below my feet. I lean forward in a wooden chair on top of a cliff, watching the waves roll in and out, as the sun drops below the horizon. I can hear Ellis walking up with the cup of cocoa that he promised peaking my excitement. He sits down in the chair next to mine, handing me the charming "Irish Memories" cup that I purchased earlier that morning at the little store up the road from our cottage.

He smiles at me as we sit silently breathing in the air and the view, captivated by the beauty before us. This is our last night in Ireland and we want to take in every drop of sunlight before we say goodbye, at least for now. We sit, gazing out at the open sea before us.

"Hey! Can we join you two lovebirds and watch the sunset?"

Kim says this as she and Alex walk up, reappearing after spending the entire afternoon tucked away in their cottage.

"Of course, have a seat and some cocoa," I say, motioning them over.

I smile at them as I think about the journey that led me here.

Dr. Flanigan warned that getting personally involved with an inmate at North Branch Correctional was the worst thing I could do, but she was wrong. The worst thing I could do would be to go through life never learning how to be happy.

www.blossomspringpublishing.com

Made in the USA
Monee, IL
14 October 2021